# SOOTHE ME, DADDY

ELOUISE EAST

# CONTENTS

# SOOTHE ME, DADDY

# CHAPTER ONE

## HENLEY

Henley James had watched him for the past six months: he asked colleagues about their families, he brought items into the office that had been discussed previously, he brought cards and gifts on birthdays, he helped colleagues when they were under the weather. This acquaintance…this stranger freely gave other people what Henley longed for. To be taken care of.

When he first began working in customer services at the uniform manufacturing company, Henley thought it would be a short stop before he decided where to focus his attention. At thirty-three, he should have known what he wanted to be when he grew up, but he didn't. He struggled to find jobs that held his attention for more than a few years, which meant his resume was not the best example of a reliable employee.

Fortunately for him, EasyFit Uniforms Ltd was an amazing company to work for. Each day was different from the last—regarding the small details of the calls, not the actual day to day process—and he had fun with his colleagues. Anne had trained him for a week, and now, she sat next to him, answering the calls as he did but laughing and joking in between. As soon as he'd finished his training, Anne had included him in their bi-monthly nights out, which always ended up as a display of drunken wandering through the streets before he found his way home.

Best nights ever.

Isaac Chapman never joined them. When Henley had brought up the question of why others didn't join in, Neil, another customer service assistant, explained that each department had their own little groups that ventured out together. It was only during big company events that the groups mixed. Henley thought it a shame because he wanted to get to know Isaac better.

It was the only reason he could think of as to why he was sat in a comfortable visitor's chair in the manager's office answering questions about why he thought he was a good fit for the customer service executive position.

The job title sounded much fancier than the job description did. The job was travelling throughout the country, assisting different stores in their uniform needs. That was the baseline, anyway. There were other responsibilities included, but Henley knew he wouldn't have a problem doing them.

"Well, Henley. Unless you have any questions for

me, I think we're finished." Derek Sanders studied him, but Henley shook his head.

"You seem to have answered everything I thought about. Thank you."

"Very well. I have two more applicants to see before the end of the day, and tomorrow, I will be making my decision. I'll let you know before you finish work tomorrow for definite."

Henley nodded his understanding and stood, holding out his hand. "Thank you for the opportunity."

"You're welcome, Henley. Now, go grab a coffee before you head back to work." Mr Sanders smiled, showing the gap in his front teeth.

Grinning in response, Henley pivoted and left the room, closing the door quietly behind him before aiming towards the staff kitchen. Finding the surprisingly large room empty, Henley trailed to the kettle and set it boiling.

Most people would say that applying for a new job for the sole purpose of getting to spend more time with another person was crazy, but Henley honestly believed he would enjoy the role. He had no qualms about spending long hours driving or travelling on various public transport, he could happily talk the ear off anyone who would listen, and he knew about fashion. Regardless of the outcome of his infatuation with Isaac, Henley knew he wouldn't let the company down.

Lifting his mug for a scalding sip of his tea, he carried it up two flights of stairs to the customer service department, the ringing of phones and mechanical sounds of printers reaching his ears before the doors became visible. He strode to his seat, placing his mug on the unicorn coaster Anne had given him as a "welcome to the team" present, and dropped down into his chair, bending forward to stretch out his back before sitting upright again.

"How did it go?" Anne whispered before returning to her caller. "Yes. Once you've filled out the correct sizes, click submit, and the order will be sent through. I will put a hurry on it this end for you. You should have it delivered in three days at most."

Henley waited until she bid goodbye to the caller before answering, "It seemed to go alright. I'll find out tomorrow."

"It's good that you don't have to wait too long. When do they want someone to start?"

Henley logged onto the computer. "Two weeks."

Anne whistled. "That's not long to find a replacement for you."

"Aww. You think I have the job. That's so sweet." Henley fluttered his eyelashes at her, receiving a backhanded slap to his shoulder. "Hey, no damaging the merchandise. I need to be pretty for tomorrow."

Anne chuckled. "Why? Do you think your looks are what will get you the job?"

"No, don't be silly. It's our night out! I'm so looking forward to letting loose for a few hours."

"Are you bringing your sisters with you? They were a hoot last time."

Snickering at the thought of the night to which she was referring, he shook his head. "Not this time. Ariel and Arianne might be double the fun, but they are also double the hassle when they're hungover. Who knew that twins would have different but equally gross results to excessive alcohol?" He shuddered in mock horror.

"You know you love them," Bernie teased from across the desk.

"Yes, but even I have my limits. I dropped them off at Dad and Pops the following morning." He cackled and rubbed his hands with glee. "Served them right for doing the same thing to me with Rebecca when we were younger. I swear I still smell the vomit whenever I hoover my living room carpet."

"Gross." Anne grimaced.

Henley slid on his headphones, ensuring they didn't mess with his hairdo or snag on his earrings. He'd done that a few times before, and it wasn't pleasant. Adjusting his sleeves and fidgeting to get comfortable, he inhaled and signed on, immediately answering a call with a manicured finger.

"Good afternoon. EasyFit Uniforms. My name is Henley. How can I help you today?"

The afternoon hours flew by, and when Henley disconnected his final call of the day, he blew out a breath. Anne had gone home half an hour ago, leaving a quarter of the staff left in the department. The company believed having staggered start and finish times made more sense with the number of calls received at those times. Henley was one of the last people to leave the building each day.

He descended the stairs as he pulled on his jacket, his bracelets jingling and glittering in the spotlights.

Henley wasn't an overly feminine guy, but he knew what he liked and what looked good on him, so he went with *his* flow. He refused to acknowledge anyone who told him otherwise. He had his dads and sisters to thank for that.

Waving goodbye to Leah, the receptionist, Henley jogged to his car, wanting to avoid the fine mist of rain. Enclosing himself in the warm interior, he decided to visit his parents. He could let them know about the job interview while checking up on them.

Twenty-five minutes later, he pushed through the front door, calling out his usual jovial greeting, "Yo! Henley's in the house!" Guaranteed to receive groans or chuckles every single time.

"Hey! I wasn't expecting to see you tonight. How are you?" His dad, Lewis, had been a sprightly man in his younger days, but as the years wore on, Henley could see that time was taking its toll. At seventy-five years young, his dad used a cane and walked as fast as his arthritic joints would allow. Never a day went by when he didn't have a smile, though.

Henley hopped over to hug him, holding him tight. "I'm good, thanks, Dad. I had a job interview today."

"Oh, are you searching for a new place already? I thought you liked it there."

Henley linked his dad's arm through his as they aimed for the kitchen, where pots and pans were crashing and clanking. "Oh, I do. It's an internal position. A step up the ladder, if you like."

"That's amazing! Well done, you."

"I haven't got it yet." Henley snorted and rolled his eyes.

"Haven't got what yet?" a gruff voice asked.

Henley deposited his dad on a chair at the table and hurried around to wrap his arms around Pops' neck from behind. "Hey, Pops."

A hand patted his arms in affection, but the voice repeated the question.

"The job I interviewed for today. I find out tomorrow." He stepped over to the cooker, placing a kiss on his sister's cheek. "Hey, Becca."

Becca smiled as she dished up dinner. Henley grabbed himself a plate and added it to the counter with the others before grabbing a pan to help serve. He never had to worry about there not being enough food for unexpected visitors. The family made extras whenever they cooked, and if there ended up being leftovers, it was frozen for another time. With them being such a big family, large quantities had always been necessary. At least, as long as Henley could remember, but he was the youngest of the five of them and didn't know any better.

"So, what was the job?" Pops asked, digging into the fluffy mashed potatoes.

Henley brought over glasses for each of them before answering, "There was a position for someone to travel and visit stores up and down the country, helping them out. It seemed a good fit for someone as socially extroverted as I am." Henley chuckled.

"Is that another name for a flirt?" Becca asked around a mouthful of food.

Henley threw his napkin in her direction. "I don't need another name for it. I am a flirt. But the position needed someone who could talk to anyone. I think I can do that." He held his hand up and smirked.

"You could talk their ear off. The problem is getting you to stop," groused Pops.

Henley pouted, forehead creasing. "Hey! I stop." He lifted his nose in the air before smirking again. "When I'm asleep."

They snorted their agreement before continuing to eat.

"Are you staying over tonight?" Dad asked.

Henley shook his head. "No, it was just a short visit. I need to get my beauty sleep ready for the work night out tomorrow." However ungentlemanly it was, Henley devoured his meal. Becca was the best cook out of them, Tracey came next, and Ariel and Arianne… well, he was surprised they didn't wither away from lack of edible options was all he could say about them. It was one thing the twins did have in common.

After pleasant conversation and helping with the washing up so Becca could rest, Henley said his good-nights and drove towards home. He needed to visit the gym, but he was too full after dinner. He'd have to get up early and head there before work. Not his favourite time to go but much needed.

After locking up the house behind him, Henley climbed the stairs as a yawn stole his breath. He strode into the bathroom, rubbing his eyes and stifling another yawn. Now that he was home, he didn't care about his hairstyle, so he threaded his hands through the longer blue-green tinted strands and scratched at his scalp. He glanced in the mirror and removed his earrings, necklace and bracelet, placing them on the counter for the next day. After another yawn escaped, he shook his head and moved into his bedroom. He removed his clothes, throwing them in the wash basket before sinking into his expensive but totally worth it mattress, naked as the day he was born.

Having retrieved his phone before discarding his trousers, he plugged it into the charger, double-checked his alarm and turned over.

↔

Katy Perry blared through the silence at five o'clock the next morning. Instantly awake, Henley sat up, rubbing his face free of sleep before dismissing the wake-up call. Knowing if he sat there too long, he'd fall back asleep, he flung the covers off and got ready for the gym.

Henley worked hard on his body and wouldn't let anything mess it up. Not even interested in the vanity side of exercising, he did it because he liked how he felt after he'd worked up a sweat. Energy pulsed through his muscles, giving him a buzz. He usually had a lot of get-up-and-go anyway, but the gym amped it up further, and by the time he arrived at work, he was ready to take on the world and win.

Unfortunately, the day didn't agree with his outlook and time dawdled. Several times, he requested additional work to keep him busy until he received a request for his presence in the manager's office. Taking a deep inhale, he danced his way down the hallways and staircases, expending far too little energy before arriving at the door. Mr Sanders called him in, and Henley sat in the same seat he'd sat in not even twenty-four hours prior.

"Okay, Henley. I have good news. I would like to offer you the position." Mr Sanders sat back in his seat, resting his linked fingers on his stomach.

Henley beamed. "Seriously? That's fantastic. Thank you so much."

"You're more than welcome." He leaned forward again, reaching for some papers. "We will get you sorted out with a new contract shortly, but in the meantime, I thought I'd run through a few things with you today if that's okay?"

"Definitely."

"So, you're starting date will be two weeks on Monday, and you will be trained by the same person for eight weeks and then given free rein to work by yourself. During your training period, you will either be picked up by your trainer, or you will need to meet him at a designated point, but you can discuss those details with him."

At the word "him," Henley sat up a bit straighter. There were only three guys on the executive team: Isaac, Blake and Leon. Clearing his throat, he asked, "Can I ask who my trainer will be?"

"Of course. Sorry, I should've mentioned that. Isaac will be training you."

Henley inhaled through his teeth slowly, hoping to withhold his reaction to those words. When he'd applied for the position, he never actually thought Isaac would be training him. He'd only ever seen Trish train executives before. There was no way on this earth he was going to complain about it, though. He was about to spend eight hours a day, five days a week, for eight weeks in the company of the one man who intrigued him so much, he applied for a new job.

If that didn't show his interest, he didn't know what did.

# CHAPTER TWO

## ISAAC

Isaac Chapman coughed as he reached the third floor of his apartment building, breathing in much-needed air. He'd let his exercise regime go after his last failed relationship, not caring about anything for such a long time. Unfortunately, he was feeling the effects now and needed to start doing something about it.

If only he could find someone like Lisa had. He smiled as he remembered the expression on her face when he gave her some flowers. The previous day, she had announced she was expecting her first child, and everyone was ecstatic for her. Anyone who carried a human being inside their body for nine months, or however long the baby decided to stay in there, deserved to be treated throughout, so he would ensure to grab her little gifts over the coming months to keep her upbeat and comfortable.

Doing little things for his colleagues settled something inside him, something that was usually centred around having a boy to take care of. Being between relationships made him feel a loss that was not easily filled.

It was not easy for boys to accept Isaac's need to be a Daddy all day long, inside the home environment and outside in the world. He was particular about the boy he needed, too. They had to be on the older side of the scale, not young enough to be infants. Isaac had attempted that type of relationship before, and it didn't fit in with his personality. Every Daddy was different, as every boy was different.

Unlocking his front door, he exhaled heavily, finally regaining enough calm to breathe unhindered. He needed to start at the gym again. Maybe it was something he could begin after he'd finished training the newbie executive.

Isaac had seen him around the office—who could miss the shock of blue hair—but hadn't been introduced until today. Henley certainly wasn't shy, which would be a benefit, but he seemed…fidgety. Isaac couldn't put his finger on it, but he supposed he'd find out next week. In three days, he would be collecting Henley for his first day of training.

Flicking the light on, Isaac divested himself of his coat and shoes before shuffling to his kitchen to shelve the leftovers his mother had foisted on him earlier that evening. Friday night was family night, and he and his three siblings and their families all congregated at their parents' house for dinner. Isaac rarely missed them, only on the occasion when his work nights out couldn't be organised for the Saturday as they usually were. Most people would think him strange for bowing out of a family dinner to go on a work night out, but for him, family nights happened every week, whereas the work nights were bi-monthly, and he believed it was important to ensure a good working relationship with those around him.

His thoughts took him to Henley again. Isaac wondered whether Henley would continue to go out with the customer service staff as well as the executives. He appeared to have a good relationship with them, so Isaac would be surprised if he brushed them off now he'd changed jobs. Not that Isaac knew Henley well yet.

He stretched his arms above his head as he strode down the hallway to his bedroom. It was only ten o'clock, but he was shattered. It had been a long week of driving to the extreme edges of Britain. Most of the time, he was able to schedule appointments that were close together in location, meaning he could get a hotel and save himself some driving. Unfortunately, this week hadn't been one of those weeks. He'd been in Sheffield, Brighton, spent two days in Cardiff and then up to York. Sleep was the first thing on his agenda this weekend. Starting after he'd had a shower.

←——————————————→

"We wanted to see if you'd come for breakfast with us."

Isaac blinked his eyes blearily as he tried to decipher the time on the clock beside him. As the number eight swam into view, he groaned and rolled to his back. "It. Is. Eight. On. A. Saturday. Morning. Felicity." Every word was punctuated with a growl.

"I know! We'll buy you breakfast, though. We're at Pete's Café on Main Street. We'll have coffee waiting…?" Felicity sing-songed the last sentence, earning another growl from Isaac, although he wavered.

"Fine. Give me half an hour or so."

"Yay! See you soon, Is." Her nickname for him made him smile despite the early wake-up call. She must have something to tell him if she was waking him up as the sun barely peeked over the horizon when she knew he normally slept in on a Saturday. He blew out a breath and pushed to a seated position. With his eyes still wanting to close, he rubbed a hand across them, bringing his fingers towards the middle to wipe the sleep away.

It was only as he shuffled to the bathroom that he realised Felicity had said "we." Isaac doubted she was talking about her husband, Van, so it was more than likely Sarah, his other sister. Double trouble indeed. There had better be coffee waiting.

An hour later, he finally made it through the door of the café to find his two sisters, chittering like old ladies across a table from each other. His sisters could easily have passed as twins: their dual blue-black hair hanging to their shoulders, and their slim frames reminiscent of their mother's appearance made him smile.

Their whole family took after their mother, so she would never be able to disown any of them.

"Isaac!" Felicity jumped up from the chair and flung her arms around his neck.

He stumbled backwards under her attack, chuckling in her ear. "Anyone would think you hadn't seen me for years when, in fact, it was only last night."

"I know, but I have news that I couldn't share last night."

Isaac pulled back, narrowing his gaze on Felicity's face. "And…"

She smiled wide. "We found a surrogate." She bit her bottom lip, trying to contain the excitement on her face that her body had already shown.

"That's great news." He dragged her in for another tight hug, rubbing his hand up and down her back as he felt her breath hitch.

Doctors had told Felicity several years prior that she was unable to have kids, and it broke her heart as well as her husband's. After attending counselling for a year or so, they had finally begun talking about other ways of expanding their family. They had originally chosen the adoption route until Felicity acknowledged her wish to have something that was a part of Van if it couldn't also be a part of her. They'd been through another few difficult sessions with the psychologist before agreeing to the surrogacy route.

Their first attempt to find someone had failed when the surrogate pulled away after a few meetings. Although Felicity knew that there were others out there, it had been a difficult time for them all. Both

Felicity and Van agreed to take a step back for a few months to reconnect as a couple before delving back into anything. Neither wanted their relationship to suffer, and Isaac was damn proud of them for it.

"I hadn't told anyone before because I didn't want to jinx it," she admitted as she dropped back into her seat. "But the contracts have been signed, and everything has been given the go-ahead. As soon as Shelby's ready, we'll start."

"I'm so happy for you. Are you going to tell Mum and Dad?" Isaac sat beside Sarah, wrapping her in a one-armed hug.

"Not yet." She played with her coffee cup, turning it around in place as she lowered her gaze. "I want to wait until I have something else to tell them."

"Understandable." Isaac smiled at her, resting his hand over hers. "I'm so pleased for you."

"Me, too," Sarah added.

"Well, you know where I am if you need anything." Isaac would be there whatever the weather to help if she needed it. If any of them needed it. "Have you told Jeremy?"

Felicity snorted. "No. He'd go straight to Mum about it if I did. He can wait like they have to."

"He's going to be so pissed at you when he finds out." Sarah rolled her lips inwards, attempting to hide her glee.

Felicity shrugged.

"Anyway, where's my coffee?" Isaac mock growled.

Sarah pushed at his shoulder, moving him so she could scramble out. "I'll get it."

Felicity hooted as Sarah skipped across the tiled floor.

"What's all that about?" Isaac asked, watching his little sister gesture wildly when she reached the counter.

"She has the hots for the barista. Every time we come in here, she's the only one who's allowed to order."

Isaac grinned. He might pass by the counter on his way out and see what he could do for her, obviously, without her knowledge. He could honestly go for a couple of cakes to takeaway. Anything for the chance to make her happy.

And he did just that. After an hour of catching up on the topics that were not parent-friendly, he made his excuses and expressed an interest in some bakery items. Sarah attempted to come with him until he gave Felicity a significant look, and she ushered Sarah out of the door quickly, "remembering" something they had to do. He'd have to thank Felicity later.

"Good morning, sir. What can I get for you today?"

Isaac leaned his elbows on the counter as he stared at the delicious looking sweet treats. Indicating two of them, he casually asked, "Do you have a girlfriend?"

The barista, Miller, his nametag said, glanced across at him with raised eyebrows and an increasing blush on his cheeks. "No, sir."

"A boyfriend?"

The colour increased as he cleared his throat. "No, sir."

"What do you think of my sister? The one who ordered for us?"

Miller concentrated heavily on his movements, but Isaac could see his jaw clenching. "She's…beautiful."

"That she is." He paused, standing upright once more. "Would you like to go on a date with her?"

Miller's surprised gaze found his as he pushed the cake box over the counter. "What? Really?" At Isaac's nod, he beamed. "I'd love to."

Isaac smiled. "Are you free tonight?"

Miller nodded emphatically.

"Alright. Meet her at Romano's at eight. I'll make sure she's there." He hesitated, narrowing his gaze at Miller. "Don't mess her around or stand her up. Got it?"

"Yes, sir. No, sir. I'll be there."

"Good." Isaac paid for his treats, nodded and left the café.

As he reached his car, he texted Felicity and told her the news, indicating it was up to Felicity to get Sarah to Romano's at eight. When she complained, he cited the fact that she got him out of bed on his sleep-in day. She soon acquiesced.

Driving home, Isaac was content. He was happy with how his life was for the most part. He wished for someone to share it with, though.

Monday morning dawned far too early for Isaac's

liking. Being a night owl made waking up difficult, but every damn morning, he obediently woke at five-thirty to ensure he had time to get a shower and some breakfast before getting on the road. Today, however, he had to leave slightly earlier to collect Henley first. Henley had offered to drive to Isaac's place, but Isaac had told him not to worry.

By seven, he was outside Henley's house. He had planned to knock on the door, but Henley came bounding down the path, swinging a backpack onto his shoulder and a lunch bag by his side.

Isaac raised his eyebrows at the exuberant display so early in the morning but didn't comment.

Flinging open Isaac's passenger door, Henley dropped heavily into the seat. "Good morning, Isaac." Henley grinned as he stuffed the two bags into the footwell between his legs.

"Morning." Isaac's eyebrows had yet to lower. He could see that Henley was a morning person, and he wasn't sure if he could handle so much energy at that time of day.

Running his gaze over Henley's outfit, Isaac decided that he fit the look required for being an executive. He wore grey trousers paired with a matching waistcoat and a light pink shirt. Small earrings in the shape of the infinity symbol dangled from his earlobes. Through the open neck of the shirt, Isaac caught a glimpse of a braided necklace but couldn't see anymore, and when Henley moved his arms, Isaac heard jangling. With the other visible jewellery, Isaac was led to believe Henley also wore bracelets. All the items were allowed as part of the uniform, so Isaac was pleased with what he saw.

"Are you happy with how I look?"

Isaac flicked his gaze to Henley, noting the eager light in his eyes. "Very much so. You'll fit in well."

"Thank you," Henley uttered. "Are we leaving now?"

Isaac wondered for a moment what Henley meant until he realised they were still parked outside his house. Clearing his throat, Isaac thought quickly. "I'm waiting for you to put your seatbelt on. We need to keep you safe."

Henley's eyes closed for the briefest moment, then he twisted to reach the belt and slid it across his body, clicking it into place. When his gaze met Isaac's once more, Isaac's breath caught. He wasn't entirely sure what the look was about, but it was powerful enough that he blinked away from the spell and put the car in gear.

As he drove towards the motorway, Isaac flicked through what he knew about Henley. Mr Sanders hadn't given Isaac a lot of information to work with, other than Henley was a sociable guy and would do a good job. That was great, but Isaac needed more. He supposed he could go straight to the source as he *was* sat right next to him.

"What made you decide you wanted to do this job and not stay in customer services?" Isaac asked as he merged onto the dual carriageway, keeping his eyes straight ahead or on his mirrors.

"Well, I'm talkative. Although you probably didn't

know that because I haven't said much since we've been in the car. But that was because I thought you wanted to concentrate on the road. Apart from that, usually, I like talking to other people and getting to know them better. And with this position, it felt like I'd be able to do that every day. Also, I like fashion, so clothes…yeah. I think I can do a good job of it."

Isaac waited to see if Henley had anything else to add to his dialogue, but when nothing else came, he smiled and said, "You'll be able to see over the next few weeks what's involved, but talking to people is a must."

# CHAPTER THREE

## HENLEY

enley wasn't sure if he detected a teasing note in Isaac's tone, but if there was, he ignored it because he didn't want to get off on the wrong foot. When he'd been waiting for Isaac to show up, he'd been pacing the hallway by the front door for at least half an hour, trying to remind himself not to overshare —or rather over-talk—straight away.

That lasted all of around twenty minutes. It was Isaac's fault, though. He'd asked the question. It would've been rude not to answer it.

"How long have you been doing this job?" Henley asked, crossing his right arm over his waist and leaning his left elbow on it as he fiddled with his earring while staring across at Isaac. He was a gorgeous specimen, and not just on the outside. Henley always believed that kindness bled through into how other people saw you regardless of your outer appearance. Ignoring his thoughts on Isaac, Henley studied him in a detached manner as he had done when he'd first seen him. Now, he was closer, though.

Isaac wore some extra weight around his waist, but his basic build was solid, so it wasn't as easy to see. His face was lined in the right places, indicating he had plenty of laughter in his life, although some of those lines were harder to see as they blended in with his stubble, which was about the same length as his salt and pepper hair. Henley hadn't thought Isaac was old enough to have grey hair, but maybe he was. It had him wondering how old he was.

"I've been doing this for fifteen years now. I came into the role straight away, without working in the customer service department first."

"Wow. You must have started here straight after school. How did you know what you wanted to do at that age?" Henley rested part of his upper lip between his teeth as he fought back a smile. Isaac had given him the perfect opening to talk about ages.

Briefly glancing across the car to Henley, Isaac's mouth curled up. "Thank you for the compliment, but I was twenty-nine when I started. I'm forty-four now." He sniffed. "If you wanted to know my age, you could've asked."

Henley snorted, covering his smile with his hand. "Sorry."

"You don't need to be sorry. You need to be upfront. If you want to know the answer to something, ask. It's important to be open about things."

Turning his gaze to the passing scenery, Henley

thought about that. He wasn't sure he could be honest about everything, especially his reasoning behind applying for the job, but he could be as open as possible about most other things.

"Did I lose you?"

Isaac's voice washed over him, and he forced himself to concentrate. "No. I was thinking about what you said. You're right."

They were silent again for a moment, an unusual occurrence for Henley until Isaac broke it with a question of his own.

"Do you have any family?"

"How much time do you have?" Henley sniggered.

"Around two hours, give or take."

"I wasn't…" Henley paused when he noticed the smirk on Isaac's face. "Funny." He held his hand out in front of him, counting off his fingers. "I have four older sisters: Tracey, Ariel, Arianne and Rebecca. My dads chose a mixture of adoption and surrogacy to welcome us all into the family. Ariel and Arianne are twins born of a surrogate, and when they were four, Tracey was adopted into the family. She was eight at the time and had been bounced around the system for too long." He didn't know the whole story about Tracey's life before she came to them, but he knew it wasn't an easy one. "Rebecca came as a surprise into the family at age one. Dad and Pops hadn't planned on adopting another child because their surrogate was already pregnant with me. But they told us they'd talked it over and decided that if they had managed with twins, they should be able to manage with a one-year-old and a newborn. And that was that."

"A very eclectic family."

"Definitely. We're really close. Dad and Pops are getting on in years now, so Rebecca lives with them, helping them out and looking after them when they allow it. I try to help out when I can."

"Sounds like you all do a lot for each other."

"I certainly wouldn't be like I am today if it wasn't for them all, that's for certain."

"What do you mean?"

Henley grinned, twisting in his seat to face Isaac. "I had four sisters to show me how to dress, how to do makeup, how to wear jewellery, what colours go to together, how to do my hair. Everything. Can you imagine me as anything but what I am now?"

Isaac flicked his gaze over to Henley's again for a brief second before returning to the road ahead. "I withhold judgement until I get to know you a bit better."

Henley giggled. "Excuses, excuses." He paused, regaining his breath. "Anyway, what about you?"

"What about me, what?"

"Say that twice as fast," Henley murmured before answering Isaac's question, "What about your family?"

Isaac cleared his throat. "I have two younger sisters and a younger brother and my mum and dad."

Henley waited for more information, but Isaac remained silent. "That's it? That's all you're going to tell me?"

"Yes."

Henley pouted. "Why? I told you my whole sordid family past."

"I didn't ask you to."

"What happened to being open and honest?"

Isaac grinned. "I thought you'd throw that back in my face." He sighed. "Alright. Jeremy is the child next down from me, Sarah then Felicity. Felicity is married to Van and has something in common with your family. They've just found their surrogate."

Henley clapped his hands together in small but fast movements. "Yay! That's wonderful news! Oh, wow. I know you're likely to already do this, but make sure you pamper Felicity throughout the pregnancy. She'll feel the loss of not being the one bringing the child into the world."

"How do you know?"

"When I first found out about our circumstances, I researched surrogacy and adoption, trying to figure out the differences and what that made us as a family. It was when I was a teenager and feeling a little…lost, I guess. I finally approached someone for more information, and they suggested I speak to a surrogate to get their side of the story. You know, why they chose to give another couple a family and all that. It was one of the things the surrogate said to me. People who were unable to carry their babies felt at a loss, useless almost, but they are the most important because they can rest and get everything ready for when the baby comes. Naturally, they'll need their energy."

Isaac was silent for a moment. "That was a brave thing you did."

Henley studied his hands that were linked in his lap, a small smile playing on his face as he preened at the pleasure of Isaac's words.

"I will say, though, my question was about how you knew I would already do it."

How was he going to answer the question without giving away his obsession with Isaac? "I've noticed you bring gifts in for people in the office." He wouldn't expand on his answer.

"Hmm."

Henley threw himself into the topic of work, asking questions about what would happen when they got there and what he would need to do. Before too long, they had arrived at the store, parking close to the staff entrance. Isaac slid a laminated sheet onto the dashboard, which Henley quickly picked up and read before replacing. It told the car park attendants that they were there for work.

Unclipping his seat belt, Henley exited the car. He left his backpack but grabbed his lunch bag before joining Isaac at the boot, where Isaac was going through several bits of paperwork. When Henley began questioning him again, Isaac pivoted to face him and rested both hands against Henley's shoulders.

"Henley?" At Henley's nod, Isaac said, "Breathe."

Henley inhaled a shaky breath, exhaling slowly.

"Good. There is plenty of time to learn everything. Do not worry. Calm yourself. I will show you everything. Eventually."

Nodding his head, Henley gave a cheeky smile. "Everything?" he asked, raising one eyebrow.

Isaac snorted and shook his head, returning to his papers, ignoring Henley's words. Henley wondered how long it would take for him to get under Isaac's skin.

When they entered the store, signed in and clipped visitor's badges to their shirts, they were led to a sizable room filled with cardboard boxes, tables and a few chairs. Henley's eyebrows rose at the sight of so many boxes, especially as he knew this was one of the smaller stores.

"Henley?"

Henley glanced across to where Isaac was placing his bag on the table. When his gaze connected with Isaac's, Isaac spoke, "Breathe."

Chuckling at the second reminder, he danced to the table. "Henley, reporting for duty, sir," he pronounced, standing tall. He smiled at the snort that escaped Isaac's mouth.

"Right, first things first. We have to go through all these boxes and sort them into alphabetical order."

Henley's eyes widened. "What?"

Isaac grinned. "Welcome to the world of executives." Isaac strode over to the first box, opened it and pulled out a plastic covered item of clothing. "The best way to start is to open a few boxes first and sort them onto the tables into piles. Once some of the boxes are empty, we can start filling them up with certain letters of the alphabet. So, a and b together, c and d together, and so on."

"Could they not have been put in the boxes in alphabetical order?" Henley pondered aloud.

"Possibly, but the warehouse works out *their* best way to get *their* job done as fast as they can while doing what they should be doing. Then it's our turn to do our best job with what we have to work with."

"Surely, it wouldn't be too difficult to print the name labels off in alphabetical order; the clothes would be put in boxes the same way." Henley opened a box several down from Isaac and started sorting.

"It's something to speak to the warehouse about when we go visit them."

Henley worked solidly for the next few hours, chatting about anything and everything that came to mind. Several times throughout the morning, Isaac retrieved hot or cold drinks for them and ensured that Henley took breaks. If Henley had been alone, he would've continued working and probably finished it all before stopping for anything. Inwardly, he glowed from the care Isaac showed. He decided it must come naturally to Isaac, possibly because he had younger siblings. No doubt, he spent his time taking care of them when he was younger, as well as now.

When their day ended, Henley had met a huge number of people, engaging with each one he could and helping them find their uniform, checking that they fit and ordering new if not. As he packed away their order forms, Henley exhaled.

"You alright?" Isaac asked, appearing next to him.

Henley smiled and nodded. "Yeah. I am. This was amazing."

Isaac's mouth curled. "I knew you'd be a natural."

Ducking his head away from the scrutiny and compliment, Henley closed the bag. "All set."

Isaac silently observed Henley for a moment before he inclined his head and indicated the door with a wave of his hand. "After you."

On the journey home, Henley was quieter than usual. The day, however great as it had been, was tiring, and he was ready for sleep. The scenery passed by in a blur of green interspersed with grey as they raced down the motorway towards home.

"Henley?"

Henley blinked his eyes open, lifting his head with a wince when his neck protested loudly. Yawning and rubbing a hand over his face, he tried to get his bearings. Glancing across at Isaac, he saw a line appear between his brows as Isaac studied him.

"Sorry. Guess I was more tired than I thought." Henley peered at their surroundings, finding them parked outside his house. "How long did I sleep for?" He turned back to Isaac with raised eyebrows.

"Around an hour. You might want to head straight to bed when you get in; otherwise, you will end up with a headache for sleeping so little after such a long day. Try not to do anything to perk you up too much. Maybe clean up and get some sleep. It's been a long day."

Henley nodded, his brain not functioning yet. "I will," he said distractedly.

"I'll pick you up again tomorrow, same time. Alright?"

Henley nodded again.

"Henley?" He focused on Isaac's face. "Go straight to bed, okay?"

The forcefulness of Isaac's words pierced the cloud surrounding his brain, and Henley answered, "Yes, sir," before he even realised what he was going to say. Eyes widening, Henley murmured, "Thanks," and got out of the car, wrestling with his bags. When they finally came free with Isaac's help, Henley waved and whirled around.

As he climbed the steps to his sanctuary, he thought about what Isaac said. He could feel pressure behind his eyes, so he knew a headache would be coming just as Isaac predicted. Henley locked the door behind him, dropped his bags by the door and strode for the bathroom. After a quick visit, he trudged to his room and stripped, throwing his clothes in the vicinity of the wash basket. He faceplanted on his bed, then struggled to get the covers from underneath him, cursing himself for not moving them before he laid down.

Thankful that his alarm was programmed to ring every weekday, so he didn't have to remember to set it, he tucked the duvet around him, resting one hand under his pillow as he nestled into it.

Exhaling deeply, Henley smiled as he remembered Isaac's words. Obeying him was something Henley had no problem doing, in fact, he relished the idea of doing it. He only hoped it would continue, and potentially, become more. From what he'd seen of Isaac's behaviour today and factoring in what Henley had witnessed previously, Isaac would make a fantastic Daddy.

# CHAPTER FOUR

## ISAAC

As the weeks passed, Isaac determined several things about Henley. Firstly, he was a quick learner. Everything Isaac explained to him was picked up straight away with rare occurrences when it needed repeating. Secondly, Henley was a social butterfly. He could coax the quietest employee out of their shell enough to get the job done with the least amount of fuss. Thirdly, he could talk the ear off anyone in the vicinity. Finally, and possibly the most important, at least to Isaac, Henley was the most obedient person Isaac had ever met. Even his past partners had nothing on Henley.

And damn if he didn't want to see how far that obedience went.

He didn't test it, though.

Isaac pulled up outside Henley's house. The executives were heading for a bar in Cambridge city centre that night, and Isaac was the designated driver for five of them, with Blake driving the other four. The bars were used to their little group now as they always visited the same venues, although alternating between them each time.

Isaac climbed the step to get to the front door and pressed the doorbell.

"Hold on!" Henley shouted from inside, and Isaac's mouth twitched at the usual exuberance.

When the door swung open, Isaac turned from his perusal of the neighbourhood to view the guy in front of him. Struck speechless, Isaac's gaze roamed over the vision that was Henley. Dressed in light blue skinny jeans tucked into what Isaac knew were Converse trainers and a white t-shirt with rainbow colours dripping from the top, Henley looked fantastic. But that wasn't what caught Isaac's attention.

Henley's face was painted to perfection. With a slight blush to his cheeks, whether natural or artificial, and pink painted lips, he looked divine, but his eyes shone the most. He had blue eyeshadow, the same colour as his jeans; long black eyelashes, darkened and lengthened by mascara; and shimmer underneath his eyebrows. Combined with the slight wave of his styled blue-green hair, the effect was stunning.

A jangling noise brought Isaac out of his observation, and he glanced down to see a myriad of bracelets adorning Henley's arms.

Isaac swallowed hard and returned his gaze to Henley. "Ready?" he croaked.

Henley beamed. "Definitely."

Isaac pivoted and drifted to his car, trying to settle the butterflies that had suddenly taken flight in his stomach. He didn't want to cross lines with a colleague; thus, he had to tamper down on all these new realisations and be the designated driver he was supposed to be.

"I'm so looking forward to this. There are some execs I've not met yet, aren't there?"

Henley started talking before he'd even sat in the car. Isaac briefly wondered whether alcohol would change Henley's personality at all. Some people became more confident—which Henley didn't need because he had confidence in spades—some became maudlin, some violent and probably other changes, too. He doubted Henley would become violent. It would be eye-opening to see the result of tonight's get-together.

"Yes, Henley. There are two you haven't met, but I will introduce you to them all again tonight to make sure, alright. You don't need to worry."

"Who are we picking up first?" Henley didn't need reminding to put his seat belt on anymore, Isaac noted.

"Sierra. Then Maddie and Jo," he added, anticipating Henley's next question. Thinking about their team, Isaac smiled. "We're more evened out now. Four guys, five women." There had been more men at one point.

"And it's Frankie and Leon I haven't met, isn't it?"

Isaac smiled, noting Henley's anxious tone. "Yes, that's right. They are great. Frankie has been with us for around two years, and Leon came onboard last year. He will be glad to not be the newbie anymore." Isaac chuckled.

"I won't be drinking much, so you don't need to worry about me," Henley said into the short silence.

"I'm not concerned. That's why I'm the designated driver. You can have as much fun as you want to, and I will be there to ensure you get home safely. If you want to drink, then do."

"I'm not a big drinker anyway, except for special occasions, I suppose. Ariel and Arianne's birthday party last year was one to behold, I must admit. Maybe I should start drinking more."

From the corner of his eye, Isaac saw Henley tapping his forefinger against his chin. "You don't need to drink more. You have enough confidence to talk to anyone and enough energy to fuel a house for a year. Alcohol won't give you anything you need. Only drink if you enjoy it and want to."

They picked up the three women before Isaac drove to the car park where he was leaving his car. They chatted and laughed through the streets to the bar, weaving their way through the Saturday night crowds to find the others, who had sent a message to Isaac saying they'd found a table. After guiding everyone to the rest of the team, Isaac quickly introduced Henley to everyone, took the drink order and battled his way through the masses once more.

He delivered his order to the bartender and the drinks to the table, and finally sat down on a spare chair to the left of Henley. As was ritual, the team had ordered shots and beer for their first round, so with a cheer, they were downed by everyone except Isaac and Blake. Henley coughed into his elbow after, following it with a healthy gulp of beer.

"God, that was awful!" He grimaced, swallowing several times.

Isaac grinned. "It will put some hair on your chest."

Henley smirked in his direction. "How do you know what I have on my chest?"

Nostrils flaring, Isaac narrowed his gaze, watching as Henley rolled his lips inwards to prevent a smile.

"Hey, Henley!" Trish shouted from the other end of the table. "Are you seeing anyone?"

"Why? I'm afraid you've got the wrong equipment for me, honey." Henley shook his head sadly.

The table erupted into laughter, and Henley received a weakly tossed napkin in his direction.

"No, you idiot. I wondered if you needed help finding someone," Trish replied.

"I'm single, but I'm good."

Henley glanced at him briefly before continuing with the new topic of conversation.

By the time they left that bar to walk to the other one, Isaac could see Henley had a buzz going. He'd kept track of what Henley had been drinking and ensured that he didn't mix his drinks. It wasn't Isaac's job to prevent Henley from getting a hangover, but he did his best to make sure Henley wouldn't feel worse.

All nine of them arrived at the new venue with little to no fanfare, where Trish, Sierra and Blake pulled Henley onto the dance floor. The rest of them found a small table with a few chairs and perched with drinks as the conversation continued.

Isaac was pushed forward when someone fell onto his back, arms wrapping around his neck and a Henley-scented face rested against Isaac's cheek.

"Isaac! Come dance with me?"

Isaac smiled and patted Henley's arms, moving his head to the side as much as he could to gain eye contact. Blown pupils met his, and he shook his head.

"I'm not much of a dancer, Henley. Go enjoy yourself."

"Oh! Please, Isie! Ooh! Isie is going to be your new nickname." Henley nodded once, lips pressed together in satisfaction at his pronouncement. "Come on, Isie. Come dance!"

"No, thank you, Henley. Go. Have fun."

Isaac pulled Henley's arms away from his neck and gave him a small push in the dance floor's direction. He might need to grab a couple of glasses of water to help sober some of the team up. They were going to feel awful tomorrow.

Watching as Henley pouted his way back to Trish and Sierra, Isaac couldn't look away as Henley's hips began to sway to the rhythm of the beat. Henley's arms rose above his head, and Isaac saw his eyes were closed, lost to the music.

"He doesn't care what anyone thinks, does he?" A voice filled with admiration, and if Isaac wasn't wrong, envy spoke into his ear.

Twisting to face her, Isaac studied her expression.

Frankie gazed in Henley's direction, a crease on her forehead as she followed his movements.

"No. A lot of people should take a leaf out of his book, in my opinion."

Frankie met his gaze, a small smile taking the place of the uncertainty. "Yeah, we definitely should. I'd love to have his confidence."

Isaac laughed at that. "Trust me, you could take some of his, and he'd still have more than enough to go around."

Frankie chuckled, leaning her arms on the round table. "How is he doing?"

"Really well. He has taken to it like a duck to water if I borrow my mum's phrase." Isaac squinted in Henley's direction, noting he had a fan dancing around him.

"You have your hands full with him," Frankie said, nudging his shoulder with her own.

Snorting, he shook his head. "Only for a few more weeks. Then he's on his own." He glanced at Frankie again, noticing the same faraway look on her face. "Is everything alright with you?"

She tilted her head and smiled. "I'm getting there. Maybe I need to rub up against Henley." She coughed and added, "That came out wrong. I meant maybe some of his confidence would come off on me if I did."

Grinning, Isaac patted her hand. "Yeah, yeah. That's what you meant. I believe you. I'm sure Henley wouldn't be opposed to having you dancing with him. Why not go join in?"

"Nah, I'm not good with rhythm. And he's coming back anyway."

"Isie! Come on. Dance with me." Henley pulled on Isaac's hand, trying to drag him to the dance floor.

"You don't want me out there. I'd ruin your… whatever you've got going on." Isaac spread his free hand, warding Henley off.

"But you're so good to me. You look after me all the time. Please, Isie?" Henley pouted, eyelashes batting at him.

"No," Isaac said firmly.

Henley sniffed and let go of his hand. "You're such a mean D…person."

Isaac quirked his mouth up at the change of wording. He would have loved to know what word Henley was going to use, but seeing his wide eyes and gaping mouth, Henley was shocked by what he'd nearly said.

His expression of horror slowly faded until Henley quietly said, "I think I need some water."

Standing, Isaac manoeuvred Henley into the seat he'd just vacated. "I'll get some. Stay there." He glanced at Frankie. "Talk to him. See if you can get some of the…whatever from him." Isaac smirked and elbowed his way through to the bar.

He wanted to know what Henley had been about to say, though, he had a feeling he knew what it was. Everything in Henley screamed boy, and everything in Isaac screamed for him to look after Henley. Thinking over Henley's behaviour during the last four weeks, Isaac could see he shone whenever Isaac gave him something to do or showered praised on him. Henley tried his hardest to do whatever Isaac wanted to the best of his ability.

Isaac wanted to take things further with Henley, but there needed to be a heavy conversation before anything happened between them. It was something he would discuss with Henley when he was sober.

When Isaac dropped Henley back at his house around one in the morning, he was second-guessing leaving him alone. He helped Henley into his house and ordered him to lock the door behind him, waiting on the step until he heard the click before returning to his car. He sat there for a few moments, weighing up his options until he saw the light upstairs switch on. Trusting his instincts, which said Henley was not drunk enough to do anything stupid, he drove off, reminding himself to ring Henley in the late morning to check on him.

"But Isaac—"

"But nothing, Henley. Do as you're told."

Isaac watched as Henley pouted before pivoting on his feet and marching to the other side of the room where he dropped into a chair and opened his lunch bag. Henley had been a whiny brat for the last two days, and enough was enough. Isaac hoped that eating his lunch would reduce some of the emotions bleeding into his work. Henley didn't show it while staff was in the room, but as soon as it was empty, he went on and on about Saturday night and how there should be more days like that.

After explaining for the fourth time that people didn't have enough time to go out every week because of family commitments, Henley had begun pouting and whining about it.

When it continued even after his lunch, Isaac took a chance. "Sit down!" he ordered, pointing to the chair Henley had used previously.

Stunned into place for a second, Henley glanced at Isaac and shuffled over to take a seat.

Checking no one else had entered the room, Isaac spoke, "Right. I am going to give you an option now, and you need to think hard about it before you give me your answer." He paused until Henley nodded. "Choice one. Keep whining about everything, and I will continue to ignore it, which will get you more annoyed as the week goes on and may earn you a spanking. Choice two. Stop whining, and I will take you out for dinner on Saturday." He held up his hand as Henley tried to interrupt. "Just dinner. There is a conversation we need to have."

Henley's eyes lit up as his mouth began to curve up into a smile.

"Your answer?"

Closing his eyes briefly, no doubt contemplating the thought of a spanking, Henley returned his gaze to Isaac's, his eyes glistening in the lights. "Choice two, please," he whispered.

Isaac nodded. "Good choice. Now, please, cheer up

and stop whining." Isaac held Henley's gaze until he nodded.

For the rest of the day, things went back to how there had been in previous weeks. Although Henley didn't stop talking, that was usual for him, and Isaac admitted, only to himself, it was endearing, and he was getting used to the constant narration throughout his day.

When he dropped Henley back home that afternoon, he practically danced to his door, turning to wave over his shoulder before shutting himself inside. Isaac shook his head, the movement being used more and more often in relation to Henley. He hoped Henley could last another four days, but if he was honest with himself, he was just as eager to get to Saturday as Henley probably was. It had been a while since he'd had a date and one where he'd have to do a lot of explaining, laying it all on the line.

He hoped with everything in him that Henley liked the same things he did, and that Henley wanted more than a fling.

# CHAPTER FIVE

## HENLEY

He couldn't believe Isaac was taking him on a date. Or at least he would be if Henley could keep his mouth shut for the rest of the week. Henley honestly had no idea whether he would be able to, but because Isaac had asked him to, he would try.

By the time Friday came around, Henley was about to self-combust. He had so many questions about what was going to happen on Saturday, he was more fidgety than usual. He was driving himself to the store that day, in a company car he'd picked up the day before. It was a bit nerve-wracking meeting Isaac there instead of having the safety net of Isaac being with him, but he supposed he'd have to get used to it with only three weeks of his training left.

As he pulled into the store and parked his car, Henley scanned around but couldn't see Isaac. It meant he'd have to get into the building by himself.

Inhaling deeply, knowing Isaac wanted him to do this, Henley put the sign on his dashboard and climbed out the car, locking it behind him. Hooking his bag over his shoulder, he strode to the staff entrance.

With his pulse pounding a thumping rhythm, he spoke to the receptionist and gained entry, following her directions to the room where, blessedly, Isaac waited. When he entered, Isaac beamed at him.

"I knew you'd be fine," Isaac muttered before waving him over. "Come on, we have our work cut out for us today."

Henley groaned, dropping his head back and squeezing his eyes shut. "Okay." He put his bag with Isaac's, listening to his instructions. His voice was amazing, not gravelly but deep, like plucking a low note on a guitar, and it vibrated up his spine.

"Do you know what needs to be done before this can all happen?"

Isaac's voice cut into his musings, and Henley realised he hadn't heard everything Isaac had said. He rolled his lips inwards, trying to remember what the last thing was Isaac said as he raked his necklace along the chain from one side to the other.

"You didn't hear me, did you?" Isaac narrowed his gaze, pinning Henley with his grey eyes.

Henley licked his lips but knew he couldn't lie to him. He shook his head before lowering it. He hated disappointing Isaac. He didn't mean to be all over the place. It was no excuse, but Rebecca had been on the phone the previous night in tears because of some guy, so he'd headed over there to keep her company. They'd talked until the early hours of the morning, so he wasn't completely with it anyway.

"What do we do after checking all the stock is here?"

"If the items do not have names on them, we put them in size order in individual boxes." Henley smiled.

Isaac nodded. "Well done. Let's get to it."

They worked silently for a change, the tiredness bleeding through Henley into his work.

"God, I'm so tired. Can this be the end of the day already? I want it to be Saturday." Henley sat in a chair and hunched over, resting his head on his crossed arms.

"Come on. A little tiredness never killed anyone. You should go to bed earlier." Isaac continued sorting the final few boxes.

"I would've done that, but Becca needed me. We ended up talking for longer than planned. Everything takes so much effort," he whined, rising to his feet. Staring at the box in front of him, he half-heartedly opened it and pulled items out, trudging over to each box he had to put them into before slogging back.

"I'll be back in a few minutes." Isaac strode out of the room, leaving Henley to continue working.

He grumbled the whole time Isaac was gone.

"Why can't it be Saturday already?" Henley leaned his arms on the box and dropped his head.

"Why can't you stop whining. I warned you."

Henley swung around, his gaze locking onto Isaac, who walked towards him, holding two cups of steaming liquid. He watched as Isaac placed them on a table away from the boxes, then stalked back to the door, putting something on the front and shutting and locking it.

"What—"

"Shush." Isaac's dark gaze rooted Henley to the spot as he wandered back towards him. "What did I say to you the other day?"

Henley remained silent because he honestly couldn't remember anything at that moment.

"I said if you kept whining, you would earn yourself a spanking." Isaac pointed to the floor in front of him. "Come here."

The command in his voice made Henley want to crawl, but he didn't think that was what Isaac wanted, so he sauntered over, trying to hide his reaction. There was no reason to because Isaac could see through him, he was sure.

"Trousers down and bend over the table."

Henley glanced at the table in the centre of the room and back at Isaac, his mouth suddenly dry at the idea of being spanked.

"Now."

Henley's gaze flicked from the door to the table before he inhaled and moved his hands to his button. Staring at the table as he pulled them down, along with his boxers, he rested his elbows and linked his fingers, his necklace clanking to the surface. The table chilled his lower stomach, where it met the bare skin. Henley felt goosebumps rise along his ass cheeks as he waited.

"We're going for ten. Red for stop, yellow for slow down. Agreed?"

"Yes." Henley felt Isaac's hand smooth over his skin before leaving. Not even a second later, it was back, the sharp slap sending waves of heat out from where Isaac's palm had landed. He bit his lip, waiting for the next blow.

Isaac spanked his other cheek this time, and Henley whimpered. The gentle jangle of his bracelets and the scrape of his necklace across the surface of the table were loud in the quiet.

"No noises. Remember where we are."

Where they were? He had no idea. Keep quiet? He wasn't sure about that either.

Each smack radiated heat through his body, and the table scraped forward across the floor, the noise piercing.

A knock on the door sounded.

"Yes?" Isaac called.

"Do you have everything you need?" a voice replied.

"Yes, thank you. We're rearranging a few things."

If Henley hadn't been trying to muffle his moans, he would've laughed.

"Okay. Let me know if you need anything."

"Will do, thanks." Both were silent for a few beats before Isaac continued talking but to Henley this time. "Two more."

The smacks came fast and hard, and Henley knew he'd be feeling them for days. He squirmed as his cock rubbed against the table with the movement of Isaac's hands across his sensitive skin.

"Hmm. Maybe that sting will remind you to listen

to me when I tell you to do or not do something. What do you think?" Isaac punctuated his words with a squeeze, sending fire through Henley's ass once more.

"Yes." Henley gasped for breath, trying to keep his voice down.

"Yes, what?"

Henley licked his lips. "Yes, sir."

"Good. Right. Let's get you up and suitable for company. We have work to do."

Isaac slid an arm under Henley's chest and helped him to stand, each movement sending needle-like stings through his ass. When he was upright, Isaac reached down and pulled up his boxers, being careful of his behind and his cock, and repeated with his trousers, gently tucking his cock away before zipping them up. When he'd finished, Isaac stood in front of Henley, holding him by the waist.

"Good boy." He cupped Henley's jaw, rubbing his thumb across his cheek. "You did well."

Henley inhaled deeply and smiled. "Thank you," he whispered.

The rest of the day passed without a whimper of pain or tiredness. It was as if the spanking had revived Henley. As Isaac and he parted ways at the end of the day, Isaac squeezed his shoulder and smiled at him, reminding him to put some lotion on his ass before he slept. He looked so proud. It was that picture that kept Henley blissfully happy for the journey home and the rest of the evening, despite it being a short one because he crashed when he finally got home.

Friday night traffic was no joke.

Apart from removing his jewellery, a quick cool shower and applying the lotion, Henley did nothing more than drop to his bed and sleep.

⟵⟶

A sting, starting from his ass and venturing wider through his body, woke him, and he blearily glanced at the clock. Seeing it was eleven in the morning was a shock Henley was not prepared for. He only ever slept that late when he was drunk.

He sat upright, wincing when he put his weight on the one place he couldn't avoid easily. Isaac had been correct. He would remember the reason for the stinging in the future. He would never whine again… maybe. Henley smirked as he stood. He might do so just to get a similar result.

But now he had to get himself ready. He had no idea what he was going to wear to dinner that night. He didn't even know where they were going. Should he go flashy? Or demure? Or plain? Maybe he needed to message Isaac to find out where they were going.

**Good morning! Where are we going tonight? I need to plan my accessories, lol x**

He replaced his phone on the bedside table and sashayed to the bathroom, brushed his teeth before heading back. Checking his phone quickly, he saw no reply, so he decided to search through his wardrobe and see what options he had.

After several go throughs and still no reply from Isaac, he called his sister.

"I need your help," he said in lieu of a greeting.

"What'cha need?" Ariel asked.

"You, here, now. I have a dinner date tonight and have no idea what to wear."

Clapping sounds came through the line, and he grinned. "Yay! Alright, we'll be over in a few. Bye!"

*We.* That meant Arianne was coming, too. Bonus. He could persuade her to do his makeup.

His phone beeped, and he snatched it up from where he'd just put it back.

*It's a surprise, but I know how you like to dress appropriately, so I will tell you that you will need to look smart, but not over the top. Hope that helps. I'll be there to pick you up at six.*

Henley grinned at the response. So like Isaac.

**I'll be ready x**

He heard the front door open and his sisters' voices floating up the stairs as they climbed, chatting constantly.

"Hey, girls. Thanks so much for this." Henley was suddenly extremely glad he'd put boxers on before he'd called them, they didn't need to see his ass moonlighting as a rescue beacon.

"You know we love to help choose outfits. So,

where are you going, and who is it with?" Arianne said, lying on her side on Henley's bed.

Henley proceeded to tell them all about Isaac, minus the spanking, and what he'd said in the message as they worked through his wardrobe choices.

"How about your skinny leather trousers with a white shirt, cinched with a large black belt. The shirt sleeves could be rolled up your forearms so your bangles will show. Then you can add some darker shading to your face and eyes to make you more mysterious looking." Ariel waved her hands across her face as if to demonstrate mystery, but it just set them off laughing.

Once they recovered, Henley agreed. "That sounds good. We'll do it. He's picking me up at six, so I need to be buffed and ready before that."

"You have us to help. You'll be fine. First thing, though. Go get in the shower and get shined up. We can see what we have to work with." Arianne stood, heading to his dresser.

After scrubbing himself raw, Henley dried off and pulled on some clean boxers. He returned to his bedroom to find the girls arguing over two white shirts.

"It needs to be looser to get the right image!" Ariel insisted, waving one shirt.

Arianne shook her head. "No, tighter will show off his body to the best advantage."

"For twins, you certainly don't have the same opinions. Doesn't the world think twins are the same in every way?" He chuckled. "All I need to do is show them you two, and everyone's beliefs would be thrown upside down."

"Shut up!"

"Hey, that's no way to talk to your brother!" he joked. He pulled on some pyjama bottoms and walked back out of the room, yelling over his shoulder, "If either of you wants lunch, I would come and tell me what you want. I'm calling an order in now."

As he knew they would, they were by his side within seconds. He placed the order with the local deli who delivered. While they waited, he made some tea and coffee. His sisters—all four of them—lived on coffee and couldn't stand tea while he was the other way round.

Lunch was spent catching up on his sisters' lives, who lived quite separately. They shared the same house, but that was as far as it went. Arianne worked in a beauty salon, doing makeup and nails, whereas Ariel worked as a receptionist for a large manufacturing company. Arianne liked to go clubbing with her friends, whereas Ariel preferred the cinema or staying home with hers. Even when they were little, their dads would receive comments about why they were not dressed in the same clothes because it was "so cute," but they had insisted on the girls having their own identity, one separate from their twin.

Once the trio had filled their stomachs, they began the long road to getting him ready. It took longer than usual because they could never agree on things, and there was always an argument before a decision was made, usually by Henley. He never complained, though. He loved that they were here with him.

Ariel had lost the battle with the shirt. She concentrated on making sure every hair on his head was in the correct place, spraying it until Henley was sure it would crack if so much as a breeze touched it. Arianne, on the other hand, made sure to make his face match his outfit and hair colour. She needed to fix a couple of his nails, too. Working with boxes did not make his manicure last as it had done before.

When he was ready, apart from his clothing, he checked his reflection, marvelling at Arianne's ability to make his eyes look smoky, yet blue. It looked like his eyes were sparkling, which they quite possibly were. Clothes were next.

It was only after he was going to put the trousers on that he realised he needed to go commando. He had never dressed privately before. They had always been happy to dress in front of each other, and it would look suspicious if he did it now.

He shrugged as he dropped his boxers. Let the questions commence.

# CHAPTER SIX

## ISAAC

Isaac waited on the step outside Henley's door. He'd rung the bell and received a female shout asking him to wait, so he stood there, flicking the keys around in his hand. He was surprisingly nervous about this date. The conversation he planned to have with Henley hadn't been vocalised for many years, and Isaac was a little unsure about Henley's reaction to it.

He knew from Henley's behaviour over the past five weeks that he was a Daddy's dream boy, but that didn't mean Henley knew anything about the lifestyle and what was involved. There were two ways this conversation could go after he explained what a Daddy and boy relationship was: either Henley would look at him as if he was delusional, which had happened in the past, or he would accept what he'd been told and be willing to try.

They would have to traverse the work route carefully. As far as Isaac was aware, there were no rules about workplace romances, but he wasn't certain. Once he knew where their relationship stood, he would make sure to speak to Mr Sanders and explain the situation. Everything needed to be out in the open. He refused to hide. Although the decision to show or hide what type of relationship they had would be up to Henley.

The sound of the door opening brought his attention back to the house. A female with striking blue eyes and long blonde, wavy hair stood with her hand on her cocked hip as she tilted her head to study him.

"You must be Isaac," she said, indicating for him to enter.

"Yes. Nice to meet you…" He held out his hand in greeting.

"Arianne."

"Nice to meet you, Arianne. Is Henley ready?"

"Almost. Bear with us for a couple of minutes more." Her heels clicked against the wooden floor as he watched her walk into a room to the left.

Unsure what to do, he followed, hesitating in the doorway.

"You can come in if you want to. I won't bite."

Isaac chuckled and stepped forward. He wandered around the living room, looking at the photos on the walls and resting on the shelves, many depicting Henley's large family at different stages of their lives.

"Henley said your destination is a surprise for him. He doesn't have any allergies, so you should be fine no matter where it is."

Isaac refrained from smiling but only just. "Is that your polite way of asking where we're going?"

Arianne's cheeks flushed under her flawless appearance. "Yes," she replied with a smile.

"The Italian on Church Street. Nothing fancy."

"Ooh, nice. I'm jealous."

"Jealous of what?"

Henley's voice had Isaac pivoting around, finding himself as speechless as he had been the last time he'd picked Henley up for a night out. Their gazes locked, and Isaac felt something pass between them.

"Jealous of your destination, which I am not going to tell you about." As Arianne spoke, Isaac pulled his gaze away and saw as she mimed zipping her lips and throwing away the key.

He met Henley's gaze again when Henley said, "Oh, that's how it is, is it? You'll tell my sister, but you won't tell me. I see. I'm going to have to keep my eyes on you both."

Isaac moved towards Henley. "You look magnificent," he stated, watching the blush work its way down Henley's cheeks and neck.

"Thank you," he mumbled, looking at the floor.

"Let's go." He rested a hand on Henley's back, guiding him to the door.

"Lock up for me, please, girls," Henley called over his shoulder as he grabbed his keys from the table in the hall.

"Sure thing." Ariel waved as they exited the house.

Isaac opened the passenger door for Henley, leaning over him to fasten his belt after he was seated, closed the door and hustled around to the driver's side. As they got on the road, he studied Henley from the corner of his eye.

"Are you okay?"

Henley glanced across at him and smiled. "Yes. I'm excited."

"You're quiet, though."

Henley was silent, and Isaac quickly peered over at him, seeing him biting his bottom lip until he sighed. "I want this date to go well. I keep thinking that I talk too much, and so I've been trying to not say a lot." He hesitated before licking his lips and straightening his spine. "I want this to go well. I want *us* to go well together."

Isaac's mouth curled up. "I understand. But I want you to remember something."

"What?"

"I asked *you* on a date, not someone you think I want you to be. *You.*"

"Oh!"

Isaac stayed silent, waiting for any questions or comments Henley might have. It appeared he was lost in thought, so Isaac didn't interrupt. When they arrived at the restaurant, Henley's mouth gaped.

"Seriously? I've never been here but always wanted to."

"I'm glad I could bring you. Wait there."

He climbed out of the car and strode around the front to open the passenger door, presenting his hand to help Henley stand.

"Thank you."

"You're welcome." Isaac locked the car and linking their fingers together, guided Henley to the entrance.

Upon entering, he gave his name to the hostess who seated them with menus, letting them know their server would be with them shortly.

"This looks so posh," Henley said, surveying the room with wide eyes. "It's beautiful in here."

"I agree." But Isaac didn't mean the restaurant. Whatever makeup Henley had put on shimmered in the lights, making him appear otherworldly. Now if only Isaac could figure out a way to start the conversation they needed to have.

"Choose what you'd like. Do you drink wine?"

"God, no. I've drunk all I need to for the next few weeks." Henley shuddered in his seat. "Water is fine. Or maybe a lemonade."

"Fizzy drinks are not good for you, so if you have one, the rest will be water." Isaac hadn't thought about his words, they'd just escaped, and he tensed wondering what Henley's reaction would be.

"Okay. One lemonade then water," he agreed without argument.

Pride swelled inside Isaac as he watched Henley peruse the menu, alternating between biting and licking his lips.

"Would it be okay if I had the spaghetti alla puttanesca?"

"Of course." Isaac wondered if Henley knew he was deferring to Isaac for his decisions.

When the waiter arrived, Isaac placed their order

and leaned back in his seat to study Henley. He wasn't sure where to start.

"Isaac?"

"Yes, Henley."

"Do you know what a Daddy is?" Henley's gaze was across the restaurant, not on Isaac, but he wouldn't stand for that. Especially as Henley brought up the subject Isaac had been struggling to start.

"Look at me," Isaac demanded.

Henley turned to him immediately, loosening something inside Isaac.

"Tell me what you know about a Daddy."

He inhaled. "Well, a Daddy takes care of a boy, tells him what he can and can't do, makes sure he's safe and looked after, punishes him when he needs it. And the boy does what he's told."

Isaac tilted his head side to side. "Roughly, yes. Is that what you need?"

"Yes."

"Have you been part of a Daddy and boy relationship before?" Isaac was curious as to where Henley's knowledge came from.

"Not in a relationship, no, but I have been to a club and had a scene before. I realised it resonated with something inside me, but I didn't like the idea of finding someone at the club. I have been sure I wasn't going to find anyone until I saw you seven months ago."

Isaac frowned. "Seven months ago?"

Henley nodded. "When I started working at Easy-Fit, I saw you visit with the staff, talk to them, interact with them. You were always so caring, gentle and considerate. I wanted that. I wanted you." With those words, he blushed fiercely, the blood rising to the surface of his skin all the way to his chest.

"How did you know that was what I was?"

"I didn't!" Henley shook his head, eyes wide. "Are you?"

Isaac nodded slowly, and Henley beamed.

"I had hoped to get to know you and introduce you to the lifestyle in case it was something that appealed to you. I didn't realise you were actually a Daddy!" He brought his hands to his cheeks, fingers fanning over his mouth as he stared at Isaac.

They were interrupted by the arrival of their drinks, but once the waiter retreated, Henley burst out, "Seriously? You're not joking with me right now?"

Frowning, Isaac leaned forward. "I would never joke about something so serious. I have been a Daddy for a long time and been in several long-term relationships. I just…lost hope after the last one ended." He rubbed his thumb through the condensation on his glass, watching the movement.

"Is this what you brought me here to talk about?"

"Yes, and we still have things to discuss. Such as, how deep into being a boy do you like to go?"

Henley's brows drew together. "I don't like playing with toys or wearing nappies. That doesn't appeal at all. But I like the idea of someone looking after me, taking control, helping to calm me when my thoughts get all messed up."

"I have noticed that you're obedient, for the most

part. So, you like being told what to do. If we try this, you will be listening to and obeying me."

"Yes. Please."

Their conversation paused once more as their food arrived, and they ate in near silence, which was strange from Isaac's point of view. He was so used to the constant chatter from Henley.

"I don't want you to change yourself for me, Henley."

"What do you mean?"

"You need to be yourself from the beginning. Don't act or speak how you think I want you to. If I think something about your behaviour needs correcting, I will discuss it with you and help you alter it."

"Through punishments?" Henley asked, eyebrows raising.

"If I believe that is the best way to remind you, yes." Isaac hesitated. "For me, being a Daddy is a twenty-four-seven responsibility. I would need you to realise that everything I do for or to you is for your own benefit. I want to help you become all that you can be, and in return, you need to trust me wholeheartedly. Telling me the truth at all times, even when it scares you. You need to trust that I will catch you should you fall. I will hold you close and protect you with every-thing I am."

Isaac gazed at Henley, seeing a shimmer begin in his eyes before they filled and overflowed.

"Come here." Isaac issued the order, and they both scooted out of their opposite seats, Isaac guiding Henley to slide over in the booth seat so he could sit next to him. Isaac wrapped his arm around Henley's shoulder, hugging him close and resting his fingers against the side of his face as his tears continued to fall soundlessly.

Once Henley had calmed, Isaac lifted his face. "Are you okay?" Henley nodded. "I need your words, sweetheart."

"I'm okay," he croaked. "I…You…It's everything I want."

"Alright. Let's eat our food, and once we're full, we can talk some more."

Isaac reached for Henley's plate from the opposite side of the table and placed it in front of Henley. Henley smiled, and though a little watery, it filled Isaac's heart with joy. He couldn't believe he had found someone who already knew about Daddies and boys, and in fact, was one.

After they had finished their meal and Isaac deduced Henley *didn't* want a dessert, he gripped Henley's hand and left the restaurant. It wasn't particularly late, and the air was warm, so he suggested a short walk.

"For a relationship to work with me, I would need to give you a routine to stick to—"

"What kind of routine?"

Isaac raised his eyebrows at Henley, waiting until he apologised for interrupting before continuing, "Things like when you'd need to go to sleep, when to wake, when to eat. I don't do this because I think you are incapable of doing them yourself. I do it because then I will know you are looking after yourself like I have asked you to. I trust that if I ask you to do some-thing, you will do it. For example, if I ask you to eat at midday, and you agree, I expect you to eat at midday, barring any unforeseen circumstances."

"That sounds good." Henley glanced up at Isaac from underneath his eyelashes. "I do sometimes forget whether I've eaten or not."

"Good to know, and thank you for being honest with me. I have seen that you can be a little excitable at times. I would like to help you find a way to manage that. I think your work, however amazing you already are at it, would benefit a great deal from you being calmer and more in control of your actions." He paused and smirked. "And mouth."

"Hey!" Henley pouted for a second before grin-ning. "Yes, okay. I know I can be a chatterbox. But I have so much to say."

"And I wouldn't ever want to stop you from saying it, but I do think there is a time and place for certain topics of conversation."

Henley scrunched his nose up. "Is there really?"

"Yes," Isaac said firmly.

They walked in silence for a few steps before Henley asked, "What should I call you?"

Isaac exhaled deeply. "I would love for you to call me Daddy. But you don't have to. Isaac is fine, too."

Henley rested his head against Isaac's shoulder, wrapping his free hand around his biceps. "I would love to call you Daddy."

"Does everything sound okay so far?"

Henley nodded, and when Isaac raised his eyebrows, he added, "Yes…Daddy."

Isaac inhaled and briefly closed his eyes, his pulse skyrocketing at the word. "Perfect." He pressed a kiss to the side of Henley's forehead, pulling him close. "Let's head back."

Changing the subject on the stroll back to the car, Isaac found out that Henley was visiting his family the following day. All of them were congregating at their dads' house for his sister Tracey's birthday.

Isaac pulled up at Henley's house, seeing it in darkness, and assumed his sisters had gone home. He walked around to the passenger door and opened it, helping Henley out once more. Linking their fingers again, he wandered up the garden path, stepping onto the porch and turning to face Henley.

"Thank you for tonight, Henley." Isaac's gaze roamed his face, taking in the glacial blue eyes, strong nose and full lips before returning to his eyes.

"Thank you for taking me out for dinner…Daddy," Henley whispered.

"You're welcome."

Isaac reached a hand to the back of Henley's neck before leaning in and pressing their lips together in a soft kiss. He sipped at Henley's top lip, then his bottom lip before pressing a small kiss to the corner of his mouth.

"Goodnight, Henley."

Walking away was the hardest thing he'd had to do for a long time.

# CHAPTER SEVEN

## HENLEY

"You're goddamn right I did," replied Henley, still seething from being left on his porch without the goodbye he had been hoping for. "I lost count how many times I came once I'd run upstairs. I don't care if he punishes me for it. You don't leave a man hanging, Ariel. It's not kind."

"You'll survive." Henley wasn't so sure.

Actually, he did care. He didn't want to get punished for masturbating all night long, but he had been so horny, and every time the images from their date came to mind, he became hard again. Even now, he felt his cock twitch despite the numerous orgasms.

He was pissed off with Isaac, that was for certain. He had no idea how he was going to face him the following day without screeching at him.

Henley knew their relationship had only just begun, but why did Isaac have to leave? He could've stayed, and they could've had some fun. But no, he was being all gentlemanly.

By the time he met Isaac at the warehouse on Monday morning, he was less angry but more upset. Last night, he had wondered if there was something wrong with him, and that was why Isaac hadn't wanted him. His mood had plummeted, and he'd struggled to sleep. So, an early morning of lugging boxes from the warehouse to a van was not the best idea. Still, it was his job, and he'd do it, even if he moped along the way.

"Is everything okay, Henley?" Isaac asked.

"Yes, thanks," he replied, picking up another box. He knew he was a lot quieter than usual. It was a mixture of being upset about the weekend and lack of sleep. He also knew that Isaac would pick up on it, but there was nothing he could do to prevent that.

"Did you sleep well?"

"Not really."

"Why not?"

"Not sure."

What he was sure about was that his two-word answers were grating on Isaac because Isaac's tone became more clipped with each exchange, and Henley felt an obscene amount of pleasure from it.

Once the van was loaded, Isaac slid into the driver's seat and Henley the passenger seat, pouting some more when he had to do it himself, without the assistance Isaac had provided Saturday night. They got on the road quickly, speeding towards a new store that would be opening in three weeks.

"Right. Now that we are away from prying eyes and ears, what's the matter? And don't say nothing because you have been sulking all morning."

Henley didn't say anything for the moment. He didn't know what to say.

Isaac sighed. "When we were talking on Saturday, you said you understood that I needed you to always tell the truth. Did you lie to me?"

"No!" Henley swung his gaze around to Isaac. "I wouldn't do that."

"Then why are you hiding behind silence today?"

Henley shifted in his seat, pushing his hands under his thighs as he thought about his answer. "I'm... annoyed," he muttered.

"That's a start. What are you annoyed about?"

Henley heaved a breath. "Because I wanted more on Saturday. And you left me standing there with nothing but a small kiss! I wanted..." Henley paused, brow furrowing. "That's why. Because I wasn't ready. I need to start thinking about both of us, not just me." He glanced across at Isaac, seeing a small smile playing on his lips. "You didn't want to rush us into anything. You wanted to go slow."

"Correct."

"Why didn't you tell me that?"

"I did."

"When?"

"Think about our conversation, Henley. I'll wait."

Henley gazed out of the window, not seeing anything as he played back their date. There were lots of talking about trust, and then he remembered specific words: *"Everything I do for or to you is for your benefit."*

"I have to trust that you know me better than I know myself when it comes to certain things."

"Well done, Henley. I'm proud of you for figuring it out."

Henley closed his eyes and grinned, sitting taller in his seat with the praise.

"I wanted to be with you," Henley said.

"I know. And I wanted to be with you, too. But we need to make sure we're happy with our decisions before we cross that line, okay?"

"Okay." Henley waited a few seconds. "When will we know that we are happy with our decisions? Because I feel happy about it."

Isaac chuckled. "I'm sure you do."

"When can we go out again?" Henley asked.

"We're going out with the execs this weekend, remember."

"I know. I mean you and me. Maybe we could go to the cinema or bowling or something? I've not been to the cinema for a while. Not sure what's on either, I'd have to check. Do you like the cinema? Or would you prefer dinner again? I'm easy, rea—"

"Henley? Relax."

Henley inhaled and exhaled shakily, resting his head back and rolling it towards Isaac. "Sorry."

"It's fine. Just remember to breathe in between sentences or questions. How will anyone be able to answer you if you don't give them time?" Isaac chuckled, gentling the reprimand.

"I get so…"

"Excited?" Isaac supplied with a smile.

"Yeah, I suppose."

"It's not a bad thing, Henley. Life is for living. If you can't be excited about it, you're not enjoying it."

"Do you enjoy your life?"

"Very much so. I have a loving family, fantastic colleagues, amazing career. What more could I ask for than what has been given to me already?" He flicked his gaze over to Henley then back to the road. "Including you."

Henley smiled. "Thank you."

That conversation, however settling it was that day, proved to be only one of two of its kind that week. They were inundated with getting the store up and running, and with two unexpected trips making for long days, they had no time to breathe.

The second conversation consisted of Isaac asking Henley if he had any toys. After clarification was needed regarding which type of toys, Henley snorted and told Isaac he had plenty. Isaac detailed specifically what he wanted Henley to do that night to remove some of his stress, and two of those toys got used so much, the batteries died. But he went to work on Thursday feeling much better.

By Friday afternoon, though, Henley wanted to cry. Isaac had been amazing with him: rubbing his back to calm him when needed, being stern when he pushed too hard or whined too much, reminding him to eat and drink, asking about his family and friends. But he hadn't *touched* him in any other way. No kisses, no petting, no not-so-innocent touches. Nothing.

Although he felt settled in some ways, he was lively in others. He wanted Isaac something fierce and couldn't decide how to make it happen. Every time his thoughts turned to the idea of pushing things to make Isaac snap, his brain reminded him that Isaac knew what he was doing. His heart didn't agree, though.

When he drove home after dropping the leftover uniforms back at the warehouse, he was ready to hibernate for the weekend. Forget going out anywhere, he was going to hide away and get centred once more.

Unfortunately, someone else had other ideas.

Henley was submerged in a luxuriously hot bath with plenty of lavender bubbles when someone knocked on his front door. At first, Henley ignored them. He wasn't expecting anyone, and those who he wanted to see had a key and could let themselves in. But when the knocking continued and his phone began ringing, he realised he needed to sort it so he could get back to his bath.

Grumbling when the cool air hit his overheated skin, Henley draped a dressing gown around him, and dripping, went to the door.

"Who is it?" he asked.

"Open the door, Henley."

Henley quickly unlocked the door and opened it wide, eyebrows raised at his unexpected visitor.

"Can I come in? I don't want you catching a chill."

Henley nodded, and Isaac manoeuvred past him into the hallway.

"I've brought some dinner. Why don't you finish your bath or shower? It will be ready for when you've finished."

"Okay."

He watched as Isaac's gaze roamed across his face and down to his bare feet and back up again. "Go on. Enjoy the water."

"Yes." Henley drifted to the stairs before turning back with his hand on the bannister. "Thank you, Daddy," he whispered, tears threatening to fall.

"You're welcome. Go. Enjoy."

Henley climbed the stairs, careful of his wet feet, and slowly sank back into the warmth. He couldn't believe Isaac was at his house, making dinner. Or maybe he was just serving it, he wasn't sure, but regardless, Isaac was in his house.

Trying to relax when the object of his affection was on the floor below him was next to impossible, but the heat seeping into his muscles did the trick until a knock on the bathroom door.

"Yes?"

"Would you like something to drink?" Isaac called.

If he answered yes, Isaac would come in while he was in the bath. If he answered no, Isaac would go back downstairs. If Isaac wanted to take things slow, why would he ask to come in when Henley was only dressed in bubbles?

"Henley? It's not a trick question." There was humour in his tone.

Taking a breath, he answered, "Yes, please."

Watching as the door handle turned, Henley swallowed hard, trying to affect a calm appearance when, in fact, his heart was racing. Isaac entered, holding a beer bottle and a glass of water.

"I wasn't sure which you would prefer."

"Water, please."

Isaac settled the bottle on the sink and brought the glass to him, crouching next to the bath. "Let me hold it. Your hands will be slippery."

Henley nodded, and Isaac rested the glass against his bottom lip. As Henley moulded his mouth to it, Isaac carefully tilted it, allowing the cool liquid to fill his mouth. Not realising how thirsty he had been, Henley gulped down several swallows before locking gazes with Isaac and lifting his head. A small drop dripped onto his warmed skin, causing his breath to hitch, and Isaac wiped it away with his finger.

"Thank you."

"You're welcome. Dinner is ready as soon as you are. Don't rush, though. Enjoy yourself." Isaac stood, turning away from Henley, and Henley felt a moment of panic.

"Stay!"

Grey eyes met his, and Isaac must have seen something in his expression because he laid a folded towel on the toilet seat and sat, resting his elbows on his knees.

They were silent for a long while, and when the bath had cooled enough that Henley developed goose-bumps, he decided he'd had enough.

"I'm finished."

"Have you washed?" Isaac asked, sitting upright.

"Yes. I always wash first and relax when I'm done."

Isaac smiled. "My clever boy."

Henley didn't think he would ever get tired of hearing that.

"Come on. Let's get you dry."

Isaac lifted another towel off the radiator and held it out for Henley, who had a moment of indecision before pulling the plug and standing up. The water flowed off him like a waterfall, and he refused to meet Isaac's gaze, not wanting to see disappointment *or* lust. He couldn't handle either now as bare as he was, physically and emotionally.

With Isaac towelling him off in a no-nonsense manner, Henley felt more secure, and once the towel was wrapped around his waist, he found his equilibrium again.

"Thank you, Daddy."

Isaac leaned forward and pressed a kiss to his forehead. "You're welcome, sweetheart. Why don't you go and get dressed—pyjama bottoms or joggers and a t-shirt would be good—and come down and meet me in the kitchen."

"Okay."

Picking up the half-empty glass and the full beer bottle, Isaac gave a half-smile before exiting the room.

Henley inhaled and exhaled slowly before following. As he passed the stairs, he saw Isaac was already at the bottom, and Henley smiled as he continued to his room. Entering his space always soothed him. Painted light blue walls, and royal blue curtains and duvet cover matched well with the pine floorboards and furniture. He loved his room. It never failed to calm his excitable nature and was the perfect place to fall asleep.

The drawers contained his trousers and pyjamas, so he chose his favourite pyjama bottoms: dark blue flannel with Tweety Pie on them. They were a gift from Becca a few years ago when she started calling him "sweetie pie," and he'd misheard her and asked why she was calling him Tweety Pie. Soon after that, the pyjamas appeared. They made him smile every time.

Flinging the towel towards the washing basket, Henley pulled them on, going commando underneath. He didn't usually wear a t-shirt when he was at home, but Isaac had asked him to, so he slid on a light grey round-neck one.

He checked his hair in the mirror, running his fingers through it to tidy it up and reminding himself he needed to dye his hair again soon. The blue colour was beginning to fade. He wasn't sure what colour he would go for next. Maybe he could ask Isaac.

Thinking of Isaac had him hurrying out of his room and down the stairs. The kitchen smelled heavenly, and as he entered, he saw the table had been set for two with candles in the middle.

"Feeling better after your bath?" Isaac asked over his shoulder.

"Yes, thank you. You didn't have to go to all this trouble."

Isaac smiled as he pivoted towards him, carrying two plates. "It's no trouble. Anyway, you know I like to look after you." He set the plates down. "Sit down, sweetheart. What would you like to drink?"

"Would I be allowed some juice, please?"

"Of course. Good choice." Isaac filled a small glass and placed it in front of Henley. "We can't have dinner out or takeaways too often, but we've had a busy week, so I thought this would be good for us."

"It's wonderful. Thank you, Daddy." Henley was feeling a lot more confident in using the word and accepting that someone else wanted to look after him. He knew his family did, but this was different. Sometimes it seemed wrong that another adult took care of him in ways that he should be able to do for himself. But he reminded himself, it wasn't that he couldn't do it, he enjoyed allowing someone else to do so *only* if they enjoyed doing it. It was a difficult concept for some people to understand when, as children, they were taught to become independent and self-sufficient.

They spoke about little things while they ate, enjoying the calm atmosphere after a hectic week at work. The closer Henley came to finishing his food, the more distracted he became about what would happen afterwards. He wanted them to take this further tonight, but after last weekend, he didn't dare to hope. Isaac turned the conversation to their relationship.

"So, we talked a bit about what I want from us. What do you want?"

"I want someone to help me be *me*, without the fall-outs I usually get from when I become over-exuberant or excitable. When I get like that, I can't control what happens. I'd like someone to help me to learn control, even if it's through obeying the rules they have set. I need the rigidity of it, I think."

Isaac nodded. "You've thought about this. I'm glad." He leaned forward, resting his elbows on the table and reaching one hand forward to encircle his glass. "What about punishments? I know you're okay with spankings. What else?"

# CHAPTER EIGHT

## ISAAC

Isaac watched Henley's cheeks colour as he studied his plate.

"I like it when my Daddy controls everything."

He waited for more information to come, but nothing did. "What do you mean by *everything*?"

Isaac couldn't attempt to dissect that sentence. He needed it broken down for him. It was too important to get wrong.

"I like being told what and when to eat and how much. Sometimes, I find I either miss meals or eat too much. There doesn't seem to be any middle ground. I also like it when I'm not allowed to orgasm without Daddy saying I can. I like it when he tells me what punishments I can take and what I can't."

Surprise flared through him at the punishments statement. "Alright. We would need to decide on your hard limits, though. That's non-negotiable." He knew

Henley needed structure in his life. Consideration needed to be given to his family, work and friends. He didn't want to take anything away from Henley; Isaac wanted to enrich what he had and make his life more settled.

"Okay."

"Let me clean up and we'll go watch a movie." Isaac stood, picking up their finished plates and taking them over to the dishwasher. "You finish your juice. Would you like any ice cream for your dessert?"

Isaac rested a hip against the counter while he waited for Henley's answer, watching as his mouth curved into a beautiful smile.

"You have ice cream?" Henley questioned, eyes sparkling.

"I do. Cookie dough or chocolate brownie? I think maybe cookie dough would be a good choice this evening."

"Perfect."

Isaac filled a small bowl and placed it in front of Henley, holding out a spoon.

"Thanks, Daddy."

His hand reached forward to rub over Henley's hair, and he smiled when Henley pushed into it. He liked being petted. Isaac filed that away for future reference.

Returning to the dishwasher, Isaac filled it and, by the time he was ready to set it going, Henley had finished and brought the bowl to him.

"Thank you, sweetheart." He put the last items in and started it. "Right, let's go see what's on TV."

The living room was surprisingly spotless, as it had been the previous weekend when he'd had a chance to study it before their date. Knowing Henley as he did, he would've immediately assumed he had a chaotic house, but the whole house was in a similar tidy condition. Henley took good care of his home, which Isaac appreciated.

"What would you like to watch?"

"Could we watch Drag Race?" Henley asked with a hopeful look on his face.

Inwardly cringing, Isaac agreed. He was never one for watching reality-style shows, preferring to watch documentaries instead, but if Henley enjoyed them, he would learn to live with it. Sometimes.

Isaac sat in the corner of the sofa and patted the seat next to him. Beaming, Henley snuggled up beside him, his head resting on his shoulder as his legs curled up underneath him. Isaac picked up the remote from the side table and switched the TV on, passing it to Henley for him to find his programme. As it started up, Isaac found himself drifting. His hand leisurely rubbed up and down Henley's arm, and he repeatedly caressed Henley's hair with his cheek.

Henley squirmed and wriggled increasingly as time went on, and Isaac could feel his erection pressing into his thigh. He didn't think Henley was even aware of what he was doing, but Isaac knew he needed rest, not getting worked up.

They watched two episodes of the show before Isaac deemed it enough and switched it off. "Come on. Time for bed."

Hope lit Henley's eyes, and Isaac fought a smile. Henley wasn't getting what he thought he was, and Isaac could imagine what response he would get when Henley figured it out.

"Head up and get ready for bed. I will switch everything off down here and grab us some drinks. I'll be up in a moment."

Henley nodded and climbed the stairs. Isaac wanted to give Henley some time to sort himself out, especially this first time, but it chafed a bit because he wanted to be the one to help him. There would be time for that, though. As he ascended the stairs carrying two glasses of water, he contemplated Henley's reaction to the plan for them to sleep and only sleep.

When he entered Henley's bedroom, Henley was stood in the middle of the room, appearing a little lost.

"Is everything okay?" Isaac asked as he placed the drinks on the bedside table.

"I...I'd..."

When Henley couldn't finish, Isaac took a guess, "Would you like some help getting ready for bed?"

Henley nodded, biting his lip.

"I need your words, sweetheart."

"Yes. Please."

Isaac smiled. "What do you normally sleep in?"

"Just pyjama bottoms. Or boxers if it's warm."

"Alright. Those were clean on after your bath, correct?"

"Yes."

"Would you like to sleep in those?"

"Okay."

Isaac stepped towards Henley, and although Henley's gaze was averted, Isaac knew he was aware of every movement Isaac made. When the hem of his t-shirt was within reach, Isaac lifted it slowly, following Henley's arms as he lifted them until it was free. Glancing around, he saw the washing basket and threw it in. He teased the waistband of the pyjamas, feeling for underwear but not finding any. His pulse rocketed at the realisation Henley had been commando all night.

"Head to the bathroom to brush your teeth. I need to fetch something, and I'll be right back."

Henley ducked his head and shimmied past Isaac, disappearing through the door. After a minute, Isaac exited the room and hustled down the stairs and back up again after picking up the overnight bag he'd brought with him. He hadn't been one hundred per cent certain he would use it, so hadn't drawn attention to it, but knowing Henley was alright with how the evening was turning out, made him sure of his actions.

He shucked his jeans and briefs, pulling on some pyjama bottoms and grabbed his toiletry bag. He waited until he heard Henley open the bathroom door before leaving the bedroom.

"Good boy. I'm going to the bathroom, then I'll be in." Henley looked much younger when he had no jewellery or makeup on.

Henley didn't reply but continued on to the room. Isaac hurried through his nightly routine and returned to the bedroom, finding Henley sitting on the bed with his back against the headboard.

"We've had a long week, haven't we?" Isaac said, stepping towards the bed and Henley.

"Yes. It's been busy, but I've enjoyed it, too."

"I'm glad. You're a natural at the job."

Henley glowed from the praise.

"Let's get you tucked up, and we can talk for a few minutes."

When Henley lifted his hips so the duvet could be pulled out from underneath, Isaac chuckled. He pulled the cover over Henley, grabbed one of the glasses of water and walked around to the other side of the bed. After placing the drink down and resting his phone there, too, he lifted the covers and slid onto the cool fabric. Switching off the lamp before moving onto his side to face Henley, Isaac rested his head in his hand, his other hand reaching over to pull Henley closer.

Deciding to reward his obedience that evening, Isaac's free hand traced the contours of Henley's face, gaze roaming the strong features. Pinching Henley's chin between his fingers and thumb, Isaac leaned down, capturing the gasp that left Henley. He was unhurried with his kisses, teasing and giving, then retreating and playing. When Isaac moved to retreat again, Henley grasped the back of his head and pressed their lips together harder. Isaac allowed it for a short time but gentled it once more before pulling completely away.

Henley groaned and whimpered. "Please. I need…"

"You need some sleep," Isaac finished, and as anticipated, Henley disagreed.

"No, I don't. I need you!"

"Henley," Isaac said sternly.

"You can't leave me like this! Not again!" Henley whined, going for the full effect with a pout and puppy dog eyes, too.

"We are not doing anything tonight. It's time for rest. Tomorrow is another day."

Henley's jaw dropped. "You're really going to leave me like this."

"Yes. You will be fine. Tomorrow, we will talk a little more, and once we are happy with how things are, we can further our relationship."

Isaac was giving himself a case of blue balls. He wanted nothing more than to bury his cock inside Henley, but he needed to think about Henley first, and Henley was exhausted. He could see it in his eyes.

"But…Why…That's…not fair!"

"It is fair. We are both tired and need to rest. Tomorrow will be here before you know it."

As much as it killed him to do it, he moved Henley onto his side, facing away and tucked him against his chest. As he rested his head on the pillow, he wasn't sure how much sleep either of them would be able to get.

"We will also talk about your punishment for talking back to me. I know what you need, Henley. Don't push me."

Henley didn't reply, but Isaac could feel the tension in his body. Slowly, though, the rigidity of Henley's muscles lessened, and Isaac knew he was asleep. He kept his own breathing steady, so he didn't disturb Henley, but his thoughts were going a mile a minute. Everything seemed to be too good to be true, and he hated that he second-guessed everything Henley did or said. Experience had taught Isaac to be careful, but Henley didn't deserve that distrust. Isaac was asking Henley to trust him, so he needed to trust Henley in return and leave everything else behind.

Henley fidgeted in his sleep, which had Isaac wondering with a small smile if he was ever still. It wasn't until he caught the hitch of breath and the minute movement in Henley's upper arm that he realised something was amiss. Isaac pretended to move position, lowering his hand further down Henley's front but not far enough to touch anything but his stomach. Henley's movements and breathing ceased. After a few seconds of Isaac being still once more, Henley began again.

Refraining from chuckling at Henley's audacity, though he should not be surprised in all honesty, Isaac let him continue for a short time. When he felt Henley's pulse and breath increase, Isaac softly said, "What do you think you're doing?"

Henley flinched violently, gasping as he twisted his head towards Isaac. "I...I..." He sighed. "I'm so horny, I couldn't sleep."

"Thank you for being honest. But you told me earlier this evening that I was in control of everything. That meant your orgasms, too."

"I know. I'm sorry."

Isaac considered the problem. If he let Henley come, he was allowing him pleasure when he should be punished, but if he didn't let him come, he would lose sleep, which was vital to his wellbeing. He decided to allow Henley to come, but with the understanding that the punishment he received the following day would be harsher. He gave Henley the choice.

"I will take the worse punishment tomorrow. Please!"

"Alright. Part one of your punishment will be taking yourself to the edge, but you will *not* come until I tell you to. Part two, we will discuss tomorrow."

Henley made a little noise in the back of his throat, but Isaac couldn't tell if it was in reaction to part one or part two of the plan.

Rolling to his back, Henley pushed his pyjamas beneath his balls and wrapped his hand around his cock with a groan, his hand stroking fast. His lip was caught between his teeth, his hips thrusting to meet his hand as his pleasure built. Isaac could see the flush darkening the skin of his chest and cheeks.

When Henley's back bowed and his head writhed on the pillow, Isaac said, "Stop!"

Henley's hand flinched away from his cock, grasping at the sheets beneath him with a white-knuckled grip as his body shivered and twitched. "Oh, god! Please!"

Isaac studied Henley, waiting until he was no longer twisting on the bed before commanding, "Again."

Henley sighed and encircled his cock, hissing with

his first caress and panting as his pleasure increased with each movement. His left hand was clutching the sheets at his side.

"Pinch your nipples."

An expression of torture passed over Henley's face as he followed the instruction, his dominant hand creating friction on his dick. He gasped as the sensations, undoubtedly, grew fierce. Isaac watched him for the point of no return, and before Henley reached it, "Stop!"

Henley's body twisted and clenched and grabbed at nothing as he puffed his way through backing away from his orgasm. Isaac was so proud of him for doing as he said. All it would take is for Henley to ignore him for a second or two more, and it would all be over.

"Please, Daddy! Please let me come!"

"Not yet. This is a punishment, remember. Again." The command in Isaac's voice was unmistakable, and Henley moaned in response but encircled his cock once more.

Henley's toes curled, his legs couldn't keep still, and his head pressed hard into the pillow as his hand worked his shaft. Isaac leaned over to the bedside table, opening a drawer and seeing a variety of toys, but also the lube which had been what he was after before he faced Henley again, unclicking the lid.

"Stop!"

Henley made a keening sound full of pleasurable pain as he let go and jack-knifed when Isaac squirted some lube directly onto his cock.

"Again."

Blowing out a breath, Henley's hand shook as he wrapped it around his length, the purple head so angry, Isaac was sure he couldn't last much longer. Henley hummed as the lube slicked his way. Isaac licked his lips as he watched Henley work himself, twisting as he reached the head. The thick cock emerging from Henley's hand was an erotic picture Isaac that would not forget any time soon.

"Please! Oh, please, Daddy! Let me come this time! Please! I'll be good. Please! I promise!"

Isaac noted the hoarseness of Henley's voice and eyed Henley's free hand, clutching at the sheets as it was. "Come."

The hitch of Henley's breath, the gasps, the muffled sounds of pleasure ramped up Isaac's need, but he refused to do anything about it. A particularly violent flinch from Henley advertised his release, and Isaac's gaze was riveted. Henley's hips bucked several times as his release painted his stomach. His rough breathing sounded loud in the quiet room.

"Ah! Oh, fuck!"

Isaac let out a breath, trying to calm his own libido as Henley finally slumped onto the mattress. Henley would likely be the death of him.

"I'm sorry, Daddy," he mumbled, the sound forlorn. "I should have been stronger."

Isaac pulled him closer, letting him rest his head on Isaac's shoulder. "You are strong, Henley. Don't ever think otherwise. If a release is what you need before you can sleep, we will factor that in. If you wanted to push the boundaries, that is another matter."

"No! I honestly can't sleep when I have a hard-on. If I'm relaxed, I can sleep fine without climaxing, but if I'm worked up, I can't."

"Okay. I'm glad you told me. This will help in the future. But from now on, you need to listen to me. No more trying to sneak orgasms when you think I won't know. I will be able to tell on your face whether you are lying to me when I ask you the question."

"Yes, Daddy."

Those words coming from Henley sounded so right, Isaac couldn't help but smile into the darkness. He had been alone for long enough now, and he needed someone to care for to enrich his own life, as well as his boy's. He only hoped Henley would last. He'd had the same hope for Mateo, though, and look where that ended up. Three years down the drain because Mateo had found someone who gave him what Isaac couldn't. The problem was, Mateo hadn't explained what that something was; therefore, Isaac had been unable to figure out if it was something he could give him.

In hindsight, Mateo probably used it as an excuse to end their relationship and place the blame on Isaac instead of Mateo. It was all water under the bridge now. Apart from a slight sting he felt from not knowing, he was over it. At least over that relationship. He wasn't over the hurt that had been caused by the breakup.

It was why he'd been so hesitant to find another boy. At forty-four, Isaac wasn't getting any younger, and some boys didn't like a huge age gap, whereas others preferred a bigger age gap. Mid-forties was a dead zone when it came to boys looking for Daddies.

His friends in the community had rallied around him when Mateo left, giving him hope that he would find someone, but after several years, he couldn't keep the hope alive, so he had distanced himself from those friends. He didn't think he'd spoken to Steven and Claude for at least a year. He'd have to remedy that— if they wanted to hear from him at all.

Not long after Henley had returned from cleaning up in the bathroom, soft snores met Isaac's ears, and he smiled again at the weight of the boy he was fast becoming enamoured with. He'd never expected to be interested in someone as comfortable in their skin as Henley was; he'd always gone for boys who were more timid or new to the community. Maybe that was where he'd gone wrong.

Maybe he'd just needed someone to shake *him* up a little. To get *him* out of his usual routine.

Maybe he just needed Henley.

# CHAPTER NINE

## HENLEY

"Yes, Dad. I promise I'm fine. This week has been hectic, so I'm a little worn out. I'll be there for lunch tomorrow." Henley switched the phone to his other ear.

"You seem to be enjoying the work."

Nodding, though his dad couldn't see him, Henley answered, "Yes, I do. I get to meet some awesome people from all over the country. It's fantastic." He cut his gaze towards Isaac, seeing him smiling as he drank his coffee and studied his phone. Henley wasn't sure if he was smiling because of Henley's words or what he was looking at.

"Sounds like the perfect job for your personality, son." His dad chuckled, and Henley joined in.

Staring at Isaac, Henley couldn't withhold his words. "I've met someone, too."

Isaac's gaze flicked to his, eyebrows raised.

"You have? That's great news! When can we meet him?"

"It's new, so give me a few more weeks before you send in the cavalry." He grinned.

"What's he like? Let me know something about him before I meet him, at least." His dad stopped to cough before coming back on. "I may need to research things if he's interested in stuff I'm not."

Henley shook his head, snorting. "You'll be fine. He's amazing, Dad. He takes care of me. Keeps me in line. Reminds me to eat." He snickered.

"He's a keeper if he can get you to eat three meals a day." His dad sighed. "Even when you were younger, you were a nightmare to get to eat. In the end, we figured you'd eat when you were hungry, or when it was dinner time and the family sat down. At least you were eating one meal."

"I ate more than one meal." Henley paused, furrowing his brow. "Most of the time," he added.

"Well, make sure you bring him home when you're ready to. You know we'll greet him with open arms so long as he's looking after you."

"He is. Very much so."

Isaac's gaze had not left Henley's the whole time he'd been talking about him, but he raised his eyebrows again with that last remark. Henley smirked. He'd have to wonder about that. Henley heard Pops' voice in the background, and his dad called back.

"Right, I'm going to have to go, son. Remember what I said. Whenever you're ready."

"Thanks, Dad. Say hi, bye and love you to Pops for me."

"Will do. Take care. Love you."

"Love you, too, Dad."

Henley cancelled the call and shifted down on the sofa, jingling all the way, until he covered the entire area. Isaac was sitting in the armchair across from him, which was too far away as far as Henley was concerned. He played with his bangles, spinning them around and around.

"Is everyone well?" Isaac asked, putting his phone on the arm of the chair and tipping his mug up to drain his coffee.

"Yeah. Dad has a cold, which has given him an awful cough, but he's alright. Pops is as lively as ever, so I'm told."

"Talking of eating, it's lunchtime." Isaac stood, tucking his phone into his jeans pocket and carrying his cup as he ventured into the kitchen.

Henley sat upright, ready to follow. Isaac had not brought up the punishment Henley would have to do, but he was not going to remind him. He didn't think Isaac had forgotten. Maybe he was biding his time.

"Henley? Please come into the kitchen."

Standing, he threaded his fingers through his untamed hair as he followed the instruction.

"Yes, Daddy?"

"I've made a plate for you. Please wash your hands and have a seat."

Henley traipsed to the sink and washed his hands,

glancing over and seeing an array of rainbow colours spread on two dinner plates. "That looks amazing!"

"Thank you, sweetheart. A rainbow of salad, meat and dairy to keep your energy levels up. It will help you when we go out tonight." Isaac picked up the plates and deposited them on the table.

They sat in the same seats as the previous night and dug into the food, Henley moaning with the fresh taste of everything. When Henley had cleared his plate, he sat back, resting his fingers on his stomach and groaning.

"I'm so full!"

Isaac chuckled. "That means you will be ready for a nap. We were awake early this morning."

Glowering, Henley agreed. "There was no need for the postman to knock so loudly."

"He was doing his job. You had something to sign for."

"That's not the point."

Shaking his head, Isaac stood, taking the plates with him and placing them in the dishwasher. "I'm going to head home shortly. I have a few errands to run before we go out tonight, but I will be back to pick you up, maybe before if I'm finished earlier."

He still hadn't mentioned anything about punishment, and despite his eagerness not to remind him, Henley wanted to know what to expect.

"Daddy?"

"Yes, sweetheart."

"Am I going to have my punishment soon?" He nibbled on his lip as he asked.

"I wondered how long it would take you to ask about that." Isaac grinned. "Your punishment is three-fold today." He stalked to the table, retaking his seat. "Firstly, you are not allowed to come at all tonight, even if it means you stay awake the whole night. Secondly, you will not be drinking when we go out. You need to be aware of everything and everyone around you and not use being drunk as an excuse to do things you shouldn't, like getting off. Thirdly, you will be wearing a plug. All night."

Henley wished he'd never asked, and he pursed his lips, wanting to argue. He'd made a promise to Isaac, though, and he would try to keep to it. Isaac knew what he was doing, and he was trying to help Henley be the best person he could be. It was Henley's job to help Isaac do that by listening and obeying, despite how unfair it seemed.

"Do you have anything to say?"

Henley glared at Isaac but shook his head.

"Use your words, please."

His nose crinkled as he withheld his snarky comments. "No, Daddy."

"Good boy."

Henley was silent for a moment before he thought of something else. "Daddy?"

"Yes, Henley," Isaac said with a smile.

"May I have a kiss?"

"You will always be allowed a kiss, my sweet boy." Isaac leaned forward, resting one arm on the table and resting his other fingers underneath Henley's jawline to tilt his head up. He paused right before touching and blew against his lips, making Henley open. As soon as he did, Isaac swooped in. Their tongues twined together, Isaac tasting of their lunch and something that was purely Isaac.

Henley's head fell back as Isaac devoured him, lying prone under Isaac's attack but wanting every bit of it. As he began to get lightheaded, Henley felt himself tipping to the side before being lifted until he was straddling Isaac's lap with his strong, sure hands resting against his back and ass, pressing him closer. Henley wrapped his arms around Isaac's neck, taking everything that Isaac was giving him.

Pleasure streamed through his body, and he undulated against Isaac, feeling his erection, hard and thick behind his zipper. His own shaft ached, seeking release. Isaac pressed their hips closer, groaning before yanking his mouth away.

"You are dangerous, my boy. I can't get enough of you," Isaac muttered, resting their foreheads together.

Henley tried to get closer, thrusting against Isaac until Isaac grasped his hips and stopped him.

"Calm down, sweetheart. We have all the time in the world."

"Please?"

Isaac chuckled. "Remember your punishment," he whispered into Henley's ear.

It froze Henley's body, and he closed his eyes and bit his lip, refraining from screaming his frustration. He wanted nothing more than to argue, but look where that got him yesterday.

He exhaled through gritted teeth several times to

calm his libido, Isaac rubbing a calming hand up and down his back.

"Well done, Henley. I'm proud of you."

Henley wrapped his arms tight around Isaac and nestled his head against his neck. Inhaling Isaac's scent calmed him more, and when he was in control, he pulled back.

"I will be ready for six o'clock unless you come by earlier."

Isaac beamed at him and kissed his nose. "Perfect."

Henley rubbed his hands over Isaac's closely cropped hair, feeling the soft texture tickling his palm. "I love the feel of your hair," he murmured, staring at his movements. He could sense Isaac's gaze on him as he continued, but he didn't waver. If Isaac allowed him to play, then play he would. One hand rested at the base of Isaac's head, his thumb smoothing back and forth while his other hand moved in circles around the top of Isaac's head.

"Having fun?" Isaac asked, and Henley heard the grin in his voice.

Henley smiled. "Yes, thanks."

Isaac chuckled and dug his fingers gently into Henley's sides, making him laugh out loud and cringe away from his tickle attack.

"Stop! No!" Henley couldn't contain his shouts of laughter or pleas to stop. They fell to the floor, but Isaac didn't stop.

When they were both breathing heavily, Isaac paused, and Henley stared up at him from his position on the floor. Isaac was braced over him. At any other time, it would be a sexual position, but Henley knew that wasn't what this was. Isaac was showing Henley that he could be fun, that Henley could have fun with him, that he wasn't all about routine, structure and punishments. Henley appreciated the reminder.

Isaac leaned down, pressing a gentle, chaste kiss on Henley's lips before sitting up and pulling Henley with him.

"Come on, sweetheart. Up you get. I need to get going."

"Okay, Daddy."

Henley felt much better about Isaac heading out now than he had, and Isaac had probably realised Henley had been postponing the inevitable.

Isaac threaded their fingers together as they walked towards the front door. "Right, what I would like you to do while I'm gone is to do whatever you'd like to do for a couple of hours, even if that's sleep, then I want you to exercise as you normally would. You told me before that you liked going to the gym or using your equipment at home. So, do one of those. Afterwards, have a nice long bath before getting ready for tonight. I don't want you to have any sore muscles from working out." Isaac let go when he reached for his coat, slipping it on as he turned to face Henley. "And remember your punishment." He gripped Henley's chin, lifting it for him to plant one more kiss on his mouth and wrapping his arms around Henley for a tight hug before moving to the door.

"See you later," Henley said a little forlornly.

"Not too long at all, sweetheart." Isaac smiled and

exited the house with his bag, closing the door with a soft snick.

Henley sighed, his shoulders drooping. Well, he did need to get some laundry on, and it was Saturday, which was his cleaning day. He had two hours to get some done before heading off to the gym. He didn't think a home workout would be the best idea for him today. Too many things to distract him.

Several hours later, Henley slid on his favourite outfit: a black tank covered with a black transparent short sleeve t-shirt, tucked into jeans, which were also black with multicoloured dragons and flowers all over them. Completing his outfit were black combat boots, bracelets, two rings and a silver chain necklace. He had styled his hair in a side parting, allowing his hair to flow into a natural wave. Obviously, he put some hairspray on as well. There was no way he'd be able to keep it looking this fantastic without *some* help.

Checking the watch he'd just clipped onto his wrist, he saw it was ten past five. He had just under an hour before Isaac would be back to pick him up. Maybe he could fit in one episode of his favourite drag show.

The thought had him hauling his ass down the stairs and to the sofa. He dropped down, snatching the remote from the coffee table and set the programme running. It wasn't even five minutes later when the doorbell rang. Henley jumped up from the sofa and ran to the door, flinging it open in eagerness.

There Isaac stood wearing a light blue shirt, which was open at the neck, black jeans and boots. But what cinched the gorgeous factor was the leather jacket. He looked fantastic. In his hands were a bouquet of freesias and a small box.

"Hello again, sweetheart. You look amazing."

Henley felt his cheeks heat with the compliment, and he ducked his head. He was usually so confident when it came to how he looked and acted, but from Isaac, who meant so much to him, it felt more personal, for obvious reasons.

Closing the door behind Isaac, Henley whipped around him to pause the show and faced him once more, a little shy. "I'm excited to go out again. I haven't seen many of the execs these past two weeks."

"Yeah, we've been busy with all the stores opening. Everyone will be letting off steam tonight." Isaac stepped closer to Henley, holding out the flowers. "These are for you."

"How did you know they were my favourite?" Henley lowered his head and breathed deeply of their scent.

"I noticed you have several pictures with them in, so I took a chance. I wasn't certain until your face lit up when you saw them." Isaac lifted his hand, cupping the box in his palm as he offered it to Henley. "And this is for you, too."

"You didn't have to buy me anything."

"I know, but I liked this when I saw it."

Henley smiled as he undid the purple ribbon, laying it over the arm of the sofa before lifting the gold lid. Nestled inside was a key chain. Henley pulled it out and held it up in the air. It was a gold circle, and the middle spun around. The centre picture was clear glass filled with rainbow colours. As he held it up to the light, it shone brilliantly.

"It's beautiful," Henley breathed.

"I thought it might go nicely with your keys."

Henley nodded. "It would look great, but for tonight, I know exactly where it's going."

Isaac lifted his eyebrows as Henley put down the box and lifted his necklace. Looking down at his fingers, he clipped the keyring onto one of the links of the necklace and dropped it against his chest. It was heavy against him, but he loved it. Every time he looked down, he would see it and remember.

"Thank you, Daddy. I love it." He wrapped his arms around Isaac's waist and snuggled into his chest.

Isaac's arms came around him, and he rested his cheek on Henley's head. "You're welcome, my sweet boy." Kissing the top of his head, Isaac continued, "Now to finish getting you ready for our night out." He pulled away, leaving Henley frowning. "You told me you had toys. I'm assuming you have a plug?"

Henley nodded slowly, remembering part three of the punishment. "Upstairs," he mumbled.

Isaac linked their fingers together and pulled Henley up the stairs. "Show me."

Henley blushed as he opened two of his bedside drawers. Both had several different toys. Isaac looked through them and chose a thick purple plug. Grabbing the lube that was in the same drawer, Isaac turned to Henley.

"Lower your trousers and underwear and bend over the bed."

Henley stood and did as instructed, remembering a similar position when he'd been spanked in the store. Facing away from Isaac as he was, his hearing picked up sounds easier: the click of the lid, the tap as the bottle was put down, the wet slippery sound of the lube being spread, the scuff of Isaac's shoes on the rug. When Isaac's warm hand touched his ass cheek, Henley breathed deeply, wanting more than what he knew he was going to get.

A cool, slippery finger rubbed against his hole, and Henley instinctively pressed back, biting his lip to withhold a moan. A sharp smack to his ass had him stilling. The finger pressed in, and Henley bore down. He closed his eyes and licked his lips, wanting to move but knowing he wasn't allowed.

"Good boy, Henley. You're doing so well." Isaac's praise made Henley fly and relax at the same time, completely at odds with each other.

After he'd been sufficiently prepared, Isaac pressed the tip of the plug to his hole, and once more, Henley bore down to allow entrance. The further it filled him, the lower his head dropped. The pleasure was exquisite. As it was secured, Isaac tapped on the base, making Henley flinch and moan. Then, he helped Henley to stand and dressed him again.

Once he was dressed, Isaac turned him around and

embraced him tightly. "You were amazing, Henley. Such a good boy taking your punishment."

Henley breathed deeply, trying to calm his racing heart. He knew tonight would be testing for him, but he was determined to make Isaac proud.

# CHAPTER TEN

## ISAAC

The bass thundered through the seat Isaac was sat on, and, not for the first time, he wondered whether he was getting too old to be out with these youngsters. Sierra, Maddie, Frankie, Trish and Henley were all on the dancefloor, moving to the beat. Next time Frankie denied being any good at dancing, Isaac knew to ignore her. He couldn't take his eyes off Henley, though. If Isaac hadn't known better, he'd say Henley wasn't wearing a plug at all. It must be moving with every shift of his body.

Despite pouting when he'd been reminded of his punishment, Henley appeared to be having fun. He'd become close with Sierra and Frankie, often texting and calling them, no matter the time of day. Isaac was glad for that. Henley needed some friends, and from what he gathered from their previous conversations, the only people he ever went out with, apart from his sisters, were three people from the customer service department. Henley had gone out with them last weekend, dragging his sisters along for the ride.

Isaac smiled when he remembered Henley's description of the first time he took Ariel and Arianne out with them. A disaster was putting it politely.

"What are you smiling about?" Leon's nasally voice spoke next to his ear.

Isaac's smile dimmed a little, but he held it as he turned to face Leon. "Just seeing how much fun they're having out there," he answered, thumbing over his shoulder.

There was nothing wrong with Leon per se, but Isaac hadn't taken to him like he had the other execs. It didn't mean Leon was awful. Isaac felt there was something *off* about him. Nobody else had mentioned anything, so he'd ignored his feelings and tried to get to know the man better.

"You can tell right off that Henley's gay," Leon said, gaze riveted on the group. "He certainly doesn't hide it, does he?"

Isaac bristled. "Why does he need to?"

Leon must have noticed the tension or tone because he immediately backtracked. "No, of course, he doesn't. I meant—"

"You meant to keep your nose out of his business. That's good to know," Isaac smoothly interrupted.

"Yes, of course." Leon swallowed and scooted back, leaving more of a gap between them. His gaze kept flicking between Isaac and the group on the dance floor, but Isaac couldn't interpret what his expression said.

He jumped when a more-than-slightly inebriated Sierra fell into his lap and wrapped her arms around his neck. "Isaac! Do you wanna come and dance? The music's fantastic!"

"No. You go have fun, though. I'm enjoying watching you all."

"Okay! Watch me!"

Isaac did watch as she careened towards the group, and Henley caught her with a laugh. He spoke to her for a moment, wrapped his arm around her shoulder and started moving with the beat once more. Their eyes met briefly, and Isaac nodded to him, hoping Henley would understand he was proud of him for taking care of her.

"Hey, Isaac!" Jo called over to him. "We're going to grab something to eat from the Chinese restaurant down the road after this. Do you fancy coming with us?"

"Who's us?" Isaac asked. As he was the designated driver, if any of the people he had driven had agreed, he would naturally go as well.

"Me, Trish, Blake, Leon and Maddie. I hadn't asked the ones you drove in case you needed to get home."

The thoughtfulness made him smile. That was Jo, always thinking about others. She would make a good Mummy to a little. "I'm happy for you to ask them, although I think my passengers are worn out." He chuckled as he saw Sierra and Frankie leaning against each other, and Henley with his arms around both of their shoulders.

Jo laughed. "Yeah, possibly. I'll give them the option, though. Is that okay?"

"Of course, it is."

Jo wandered off to the dancefloor, and Isaac watched the animated conversation. He had a feeling Sierra would want to go, but Frankie and Henley appeared to have had enough. Sierra was completely off her face, so he didn't think it wise. Jo strode back to him.

"Sierra wanted to stay, but I persuaded her to go home instead. She's wasted. And Frankie and Henley were happy to go home."

"Thanks, Jo. We'll bow out this time. But next time you decide to, we'll be there."

"Alright. Do you need any help getting them into the car?"

"No, don't worry. Henley hasn't been drinking, so he'll help me."

"Yeah, what's up with that? Last time, he was sozzled." Leon chuckled.

Isaac assumed it was an attempt at a joke. "Henley doesn't need to drink to have a good time, unlike some people," Isaac all but snarled at him. He could see Leon was on his way to the land of unpleasant mornings. Maybe that was the cause for his words earlier.

Leon stared at Isaac, making him second-guess his opinion of how drunk he was until Leon giggled like a small child. Isaac shook his head and ignored him. When he turned back to the dance floor, he saw the group walking towards him, or rather Henley and Frankie holding Sierra between them. Isaac stood quickly.

"We'll say goodbye now, folks," Isaac called to the rest of the group. "Thanks for the great night. We'll see you soon, or in two weeks, depending on how busy we all are." He waved.

"Night, guys and gals," Henley added.

"Let's get these two to the car." Isaac pointed at Sierra and Frankie, and they each took one woman. Frankie was less drunk but not by much. Isaac heard her jabbering away to Henley, and Henley softly answering her, but the music was too loud for him to hear what was said. When they exited the bar, Isaac's ears were ringing.

He led the way to his car and helped Sierra sit in the back seat, buckling her in tight. Henley did the same with Frankie, and they both got in the front.

"Well, that was an interesting night." Henley laughed.

"I find it's always more interesting and amusing when you're sober." Isaac grinned. "And there are fewer consequences, too."

"True that."

"Did you have a good time?" Henley had appeared to enjoy himself, but he wanted to be certain. He needed to know if drinking was a game-changer for Henley or not.

"It was great," he said enthusiastically. "I love that bar. It's one of my regulars when I go out with my sisters. We also go to that Chinese place that they talked about. The food there is delicious. Do you think we could maybe get something to eat when we get home?"

Henley's eyes grew round as he realised what he'd said, and he quickly glanced in the back seat.

Isaac grinned. "I think you're okay. They look like they're asleep."

"God, I'm so sorry. I didn't think. I just spewed."

"Yes, we don't want spewing of any kind in my car, thanks," Isaac replied, straight-faced.

Henley was quiet for a moment before snickering quietly. "I can't guarantee that," he sputtered.

"Let's hope they sleep the whole journey home."

"If they do, be ready to open the door quickly when we stop."

"Why?" Isaac asked, brows drawn low.

"Because the motion of the car coming to a stop is more likely to cause sickness than anything else. Their brain still thinks they're moving even though they aren't. Mixed brain signals usually mean vomiting."

"Who taught you that?"

"Dad and Pops. They taught us how to look after each other and look out for symptoms of all manners of things. It helped on more than one occasion." He chuckled.

"Full of surprises," Isaac muttered.

They dropped Sierra off first, and as Henley predicted, she vomited within seconds of the car stopping. Luckily, Isaac had listened to Henley and jumped out, opening the car door immediately. And also, luckily, the vomit landed on the path, not in his car. Isaac deposited Sierra into the loving arms of her husband and bid goodnight.

Frankie lived several streets away from Sierra, so it didn't take long for her to be home and left with her waiting girlfriend. Isaac saw Henley's eyebrows rise, but he said nothing until they were in the car.

After they had been driving a few minutes, Henley said, "Why didn't you tell me Frankie was a transwoman?"

Isaac didn't miss a beat. "It's not my place to say. It's up to Frankie who she trusts with her information. You should be honoured that she gave that much of herself to you."

"Oh, I am! Don't get me wrong. I meant…"

He trailed off, and Isaac allowed him time to think through what he was going to say.

"Yeah, you're right. I shouldn't have assumed you'd spill all the beans about everyone. I wouldn't want people talking about me behind my back, so why should I expect you to tell me those things?" He ducked his head. "Sorry, Daddy."

"You have nothing to be sorry for. I could see you were thinking about why you had made the assumption, and you came to the right conclusion. I can't ask for more than that from you." Isaac laid his hand on Henley's thigh and squeezed. "I'm proud of you."

Henley grinned as Isaac knew he would and concentrated on driving. Not to Henley's home, though. When Isaac parked the car in the designated parking area for the apartment building, Henley's forehead was furrowed as he inspected his surroundings.

"Where are we?"

"My place."

Henley's head whipped around to Isaac. "Seriously?" he asked with a grin.

Isaac nodded, barely containing his own smile as Henley's exuberance began to shine through.

Clapping his hands together, Henley exited the car, uncaring of the brisk breeze, and danced around the car to Isaac. "I can't wait to see it."

"Well, you haven't got much longer, sweetheart."

"What floor are you on?"

"Three."

Henley grabbed Isaac's hand and followed in his wake as he guided them to his front door. Unlocking it, he waved his hand for Henley to enter first. He had nothing to hide. Henley practically skipped into the apartment, stopping before the step down into the living area.

Isaac removed his leather coat, hanging it on a peg beside the door and toed off his boots. When Henley had still not said a word, he ambled to his side and cocked his head at him. "Problem?"

Henley shook his head slowly.

"It's not often I've seen you speechless. What are you thinking, sweetheart?" Isaac moved behind Henley, gripping his thin denim jacket and pulling it off his shoulders. He moved to hang it up, then returned, bending down to remove Henley's boots, which took a little longer with the number of laces he had. When Henley was finally free of them, Isaac placed them next to his own, thinking how good they looked together, and he returned once more to Henley's side.

"It's gorgeous," Henley breathed, gaze slowly roaming across the space.

Isaac tried to study the area as if he'd never seen it before. It was an open plan, apart from two bedrooms and a bathroom. In front of them was the dining area, where the table and chairs were—not often used, he had to admit. To their immediate left was a large kitchen with a squared breakfast bar dividing the kitchen from the dining area. Looking between the two spaces and into the far corner of the apartment was a lowered living area that you had to step down into. It was a large space with a corner window as well as windows running the length of the whole apartment. The natural light he received was phenomenal.

When Isaac had purchased the apartment many, many years ago, he'd received an amazing deal on it. He wouldn't want to move and leave the views any time soon. Tomorrow, he might be able to show Henley the sunrise.

"Right, Mr James. Let's get you ready for bed." Isaac smoothed a hand along Henley's back and pressed against his spine to move him away from the view and towards the bedroom. His bedroom door was already open, so he reached in to switch the light on and indicated for Henley to go first.

"I knew you liked blue," Henley stated.

Caught off guard by the random comment, Isaac chuffed. "Yes, I do. Why do you say that?" Isaac made his way over to the drawers and removed his watch before turning and bracing his back against it as he watched Henley wander around the room.

"You always seem to have something blue on you. Either a shirt, a suit, or a tie. Something blue. Now, I find your room is blue, as well. Is that your favourite colour, Daddy?"

"Yes, sweetheart, the blue of your eyes, especially." Isaac stared at him, wondering how he got so lucky. He would love nothing more than to make love to Henley, but he couldn't. Not tonight. He had to be firm with his punishments, or Henley would rebel every time. "Come here."

Henley glanced over at him and changed direction, sashaying his way across the floor until he was close enough for Isaac to grab his belt hooks and pull him close. He could feel Henley's hard cock between them. Isaac dipped his head, pausing before he kissed Henley to get lost in those glacial pools, then fused their lips together. He planned to make things a little more difficult for Henley, and he couldn't resist his mouth any longer.

Sipping, licking and nibbling at Henley's lips, Isaac groaned when he was given entrance. Isaac used his tongue to explore every inch of Henley's mouth as his hands roamed across every inch of Henley's body, pressing against the plug when he reached his ass, causing Henley to moan. Henley was trying to pull their clothes off, but Isaac held firm. Henley probably hadn't remembered his punishment, and if he became any more aroused, Isaac would bear the brunt of Henley being awake and pouting all night.

Gentling the kiss, Isaac pulled away, both were breathing heavily.

"Why did you stop?" Henley asked.

"Because it's time for bed." As Isaac knew he would, Henley scowled, so Isaac reminded him once more. "Remember your punishment."

Henley's mouth dropped open, and he spluttered, but sighed and dropped his shoulders. "Yes, Daddy."

"Good boy. Let's get cleaned up. I have spare toiletries and some boxers you can wear for tonight."

Isaac turned and opened the top drawer, finding the smaller sizes he had worn several years ago but had not touched as much lately. They might be too big for Henley, but they would work for now. He strode into the bathroom with Henley following. It was big enough for the two of them to stand comfortably without being unable to manoeuvre.

"Let's get you changed first. Arms up." Isaac grabbed the hem of Henley's t-shirt and lifted it off, making sure his necklace didn't get tangled. "And again." He did the same thing with the tank top. Having Henley's naked chest right in front of him was as much torture for Isaac as it was for Henley to have to wait to come.

The buttons on Henley's jeans came undone easily, and Isaac pulled them and his briefs down at the same time, dropping to his knees to help Henley step out of them. As he reached for the boxers to slip on, Henley's cock stood proud, inches from his mouth. He licked his lips and swallowed, tearing his gaze away when Henley's hand gripped the base of his shaft.

# CHAPTER ELEVEN

## HENLEY

"Sorry, I'm trying not to come. It's difficult when you look at me like that!" Henley's voice was pained, and his eyes were screwed tightly shut.

"Foot up." Isaac tapped his left foot, hooking the boxers over, and tapped the right foot before repeating. He slid the material up Henley's legs but stopped short of tucking his cock away. "Hands resting on the bath, legs spread."

Henley swallowed and obeyed, opening himself for Isaac. He couldn't see him, but Isaac's hands were smoothing across his skin until one hand gripped the base of the plug. Isaac twisted it around a couple of times before pulling on it and slowly withdrawing it from Henley's highly-strung body. Henley gasped and tried to breathe through the sensations, gritting his teeth against the need to come when the plug finally came free, and he slumped forward.

"Stand up."

Legs wobbling, Henley stood as best he could, and Isaac twisted him around. Reaching for the boxers, Isaac slid them up and over his angry looking cock. "Right, let's wash up. There are spare toothbrushes under here." He opened the cupboard under the sink and backed away from him. "Go ahead and come out when you're finished."

Isaac shut the door as he left, giving Henley a chance to calm down.

Henley inhaled then exhaled slowly. Resting his hands on the sink, he hung his head. It was going to be a long torturous night. He was tempted to stroke himself to completion right now and get it over with, but the thought of disappointing his Daddy made him reconsider.

Straightening up, he glanced in the mirror, seeing the tension bracketing his face. His eyes caught on the chain still encircling his neck, and he lifted the rainbow, spinning the centre around and around. It was beautiful the way the light caught the different colours. He unclipped the chain, setting it aside, slid off each of the bangles and rings and left them in a pile on the counter. He washed up and brushed his teeth before setting everything back down.

One more deep breath centred him, so he took a chance and left the bathroom, entering the empty bedroom. He could hear running water and assumed Isaac was in the other bathroom, getting ready for bed. Now that he was alone in the room, Henley felt a little unsure of himself. He didn't want to get into bed without Isaac being there. Which was probably a silly thing to worry about, but it was Isaac's house, after all.

When Isaac entered the bedroom, Henley waited at the end of the bed.

"Everything okay?" Isaac asked as he slipped off his shirt.

"Yes, Daddy. I wasn't sure which side you slept on, so I didn't want to take your space," Henley uttered, eyes captivated.

"I'd like it if you could sleep on the left."

Henley nodded, smiling as he relaxed in Isaac's presence, and walked over to slide under the covers. He knew Isaac was watching him as he got comfortable, and Henley stared at Isaac as Isaac studied him, a bit like a bug under a microscope.

Shaking his head as if pulling himself from a dream, Isaac pointed to the bedside table. "I brought some water for you in case you were thirsty." He wandered over to the bed, lifting the covers and crawling in next to Henley. The minute he was situated, Isaac lifted his arm for Henley to snuggle in, and they both sighed.

"You do realise I probably won't be able to sleep, don't you?" Henley whispered, his hard shaft pressing against Isaac's hip.

"Hopefully, you will, but if you don't, I'll keep you company."

Henley ran his hand up and down Isaac's chest, loving the feel of the minimal hair which would feel amazing against his skin. He'd had a fantastic night, even without the alcohol. It was one of the only times he'd been out and not thrown back at least one alcoholic drink. He hadn't minded, surprisingly. Sierra and Frankie were fantastic, and when Frankie had admitted, drunkenly, that she was a transwoman, it had shocked him initially but had no bearing on her as a person. He would have to tread carefully when he next saw her, though. She may not remember telling him.

Losing himself in the feeling of being so close to Isaac and in the rhythmic stroking of Isaac's hand on his upper arm, he relaxed further.

Movement woke him, and he groaned, rolling over onto his other side and burrowing into the pillow. When a chuckle reached his ear, he blearily opened his eyes a fraction, seeing Isaac facing him with his head rested in his hands.

"Good morning, sweetheart." Isaac ran his fingers down the side of Henley's face before cupping his jaw and lifting him to Isaac's kiss.

Henley groaned once more, pressing closer, wanting more. Isaac smiled against his lips and licked the seam of Henley's mouth, demanding entry. Henley granted him access, and Isaac pushed forward, forcing Henley onto his back as the kiss went from nought to sixty in seconds. Maybe they were both feeling the lack of activity the previous night, but this morning all bets were off.

Isaac slid a leg in between Henley's thighs, pressing up to massage against his balls and cock. Henley moaned into Isaac's mouth and wrapped his arms around Isaac's neck, keeping them as close as humanly possible. Isaac's hands were roaming all over Henley's body, skimming across his skin, leaving goosebumps and heat trails in his wake. It was all Henley could do to hold on and take whatever Isaac dished out.

Henley's rock-hard shaft gained friction from being squashed between their bodies, and he didn't think he was going to last long.

Isaac pulled off, both gasping for breath, and reached for the drawer in the bedside table. Henley couldn't help but keep thrusting against Isaac's stomach until his Daddy's voice demanded he stopped. Visibly shaking with restraint, Henley gripped the sheets below him as Isaac lifted to his knees, lube held in his hand.

Sighing with relief, Henley spread his legs and licked his lips as he eyed the container and the person holding it.

"Now we're going to take this slowly this first time, Henley. I want the first time that we come together to be amazing for us both. Try to be patient," Isaac remarked.

"Yes, Daddy," Henley whispered.

"Good boy. Let me see you more. Lift your legs a little higher." Henley did so. "Great. Wow, look at you," Isaac said with awe in his voice. Isaac ran a finger from his taint to his hole, and Henley fought not to react, except for a gasping inhale. "You're gorgeous, even here." He slid onto his stomach, his face level with Henley's ass, which Henley felt clench in response. "So eager to have something in here." Isaac rubbed a circle around his hole without penetrating. "Grip the backs of your thighs. I want a taste."

Henley's eyes rolled into the back of his head as he did as he was told, exposing himself completely to Isaac. Exquisite torture followed as Isaac licked a stripe down from his balls and ending at his hole. Isaac proceeded to lap at it repeatedly before firming his tongue and pressing against the rim several times. Isaac returned to lapping, more pressure than before, then stuck his tongue in Henley's hole again, withdrawing and entering, withdrawing and entering.

Henley was out of his mind. He'd been rimmed before, but nothing like this. He slammed his head back against the pillow when Isaac raked his teeth over the area in gentle bites before licking at him again.

When Isaac pulled back, Henley whimpered, but a cool finger replaced Isaac's mouth. When Isaac had lubed it, Henley had no idea, blissed out as he was, but he no longer cared when said finger was inserted into his hole. Henley gasped as pleasure began tingling up and down his spine. A second then a third finger quickly followed, Henley humming with delight at the stretch he felt. The stretch he always associated with pleasure that was soon to follow.

As the fingers left him bereft, Isaac rose to his knees once more. He ripped open a condom packet with his teeth and deftly rolled it on before smearing it with lube. Bracing one hand next to Henley's head, the other guiding his cock, Isaac lifted his gaze to Henley.

"You still with me, Henley?" Isaac's voice was strained and deep, the tension in his shoulders belying his control.

Henley nodded emphatically. "Please! Please! I want you so bad!"

"You have been such a good boy, Henley."

With those words, Isaac sank slowly but without stopping until he was balls deep. He leaned down onto his forearms and cupped Henley's head. Henley lifted his legs and wrapped them around Isaac's lower back, crossing his ankles, repeating it with his arms around Isaac's upper back.

"Henley." Isaac's tone was reverent as his lips teased Henley's mouth.

Wound around each other as they were meant to be, Isaac could only move in small increments, which he did. His hips pulled back before flexing forward over and over as his mouth and tongue explored Henley's mouth.

As their pleasure grew, Henley loosened his legs, resting his feet back on the bed, allowing Isaac more room. As if that was his cue, Isaac rose onto his hands, bracing himself as his hips snapped forward, deeper and harder than before.

"Wrap your hand around your cock, sweetheart."

Henley blinked up at him and encircled his dripping shaft. He gasped at the arousal spiralling through his body.

"That's it." Isaac shifted his hands, so Henley's legs were resting on his forearms, opening him up further.

"Fuck! Daddy! Please, let me come!" Henley panted.

Isaac pounded into Henley, leaning forward to seal

their lips together in a brief kiss before lifting and grunting, "Come, Henley."

Isaac hadn't even finished speaking when Henley keened through his climax. As he came down from his high, he felt Isaac's rhythm falter before he bellowed Henley's name and snapped his hips forward one more time before stilling. After what felt like an age, Isaac relaxed, gasping heavily and, holding onto the condom, withdrew with a wince from Henley.

As Isaac crawled off the bed, he murmured, "You're going to be the death of me." To which, Henley grinned.

"In such a nice way, though."

Isaac snorted and disappeared into the bathroom, returning with a damp, warm cloth. He carefully wiped Henley's ass, balls, stomach and sensitive cock then threw it into the wash basket. Climbing back into bed, Isaac opened his arms for Henley, who turned and snuggled into what was fast becoming his favourite position. Isaac pulled the covers over them and wrapped Henley tight.

"Thank you, Daddy."

"What for?" Isaac pressed a kiss to the top of Henley's head.

"For taking care of me. I think that helped me to fall asleep last night. Usually, if I am worked up and hard, I wouldn't be able to think about anything else, making the night so long unless I did something about it. But with you...I felt content. I knew I would be fine."

"That's my job, sweet boy. To care for you, and I love that I can do that for you."

⟷

"Henley? Can I speak to you, please?" Mr Sanders leaned down close to where Henley was sitting in the office. They had been back from the warehouse for a little over half an hour when Isaac was called into the manager's office. Ten minutes ago, he came storming out of the room, face looking like thunder, and walked straight out of the office without saying anything.

"Sure. Is everything okay?"

"Let's speak in my office, please."

Henley followed him to the spacious room with several large windows overlooking the surrounding trees. Where the office was based was on the edge of an industrial estate, and the trees were there to offset the environmental effects of having the buildings there. Almost as if the companies were apologising to the earth for taking over nature.

As he sat, he noticed Mr Sanders leaning his elbows against his desk with a frown on his face.

"Henley. There has been a claim of sexual harassment against Isaac."

"What! No way! He—"

"The claimant says *you* are the victim."

Henley was stunned to silence, his mouth gaping as he gawked at his boss.

"I can see that has shocked you."

Henley snorted. "Yeah, a little. Who would say that? And why?"

"I need to ask you a few questions." Henley nodded. "Has Isaac ever made any sexual advances towards you that you did not wish for?"

Trying to withhold his smirk at how the question was phrased, Henley swallowed before answering, "None that were not wanted."

Mr Sanders smiled. "Are you in a relationship with Isaac?"

Henley grimaced. As far as he knew, there were no rules about colleagues dating, but he was hesitant to get them into trouble if he'd missed something. He had to go with the truth, though. "Yes."

His boss nodded. "Thank you for being honest. As you are probably aware, it is not against the rules, though, we request that PDA's are kept to a minimum. I've spoken to Isaac, who, understandably, is upset about the claim. I must admit, I had never put much faith in it, but I had to follow the protocol. I have a feeling the claimant has an axe to grind against Isaac, so keep an eye on him for me."

Henley blew out a breath. "Who would do that to him? Isaac has never hurt anyone. He is probably the best of all of us."

"You're right there, which is another reason why I was so uneasy about the claim." His boss sighed. "I told Isaac he wasn't allowed to speak with you before I did, which is probably why he stormed out of the office. So, I permit you to grab all your stuff—yours and his—and head home. Forget about work for the rest of the day. I will be dealing with the claimant anyway, so it would be better if you weren't around."

"Yes, sir. And thank you for believing in Isaac."

Mr Sanders grinned. "He's a good one. Keep tight hold of him."

"I plan to," Henley replied with a laugh.

Henley exited the office to find several eyes tracking his movements, but he ignored them all. He switched off his laptop after saving what he'd been working on, did the same to Isaac's laptop, closed them both down and placed them in their bags. Flinging both bags over his shoulders, grabbing their lunch bags and coats, he felt like a packhorse, but he headed out of the office to find Isaac. First stop was at the car, which was where he hoped to find Isaac.

And he was correct. The passenger door was wide open, and Isaac was sitting sideways in the seat with his feet on the ground outside, elbows on his thighs, head in his hands.

"Hey, troublemaker," Henley spoke softly so as not to make Isaac jump. When there was no response, he moved to stand in front of him, carefully setting the bags on the ground next to his feet, then crouched down, resting his hands on Isaac's clenched ones.

"Who would do that?" Isaac's tone caused Henley's heart to break. Whoever thought that this man in front of him could harm a fly was well out of order.

"No one who matters. I straightened it all out with Mr Sanders. He knows we are in a relationship, and he's happy with it."

Isaac peeked up at him at that. "He is?"

Henley nodded. "Yep. Even told me to keep tight hold of you and never let you go." He smirked. "It was part of my plan all along so…" He shrugged. "Oh, and bonus, he let us finish work already. So, we can head home. Whatever will we do with ourselves?" He waggled his eyebrows up and down and stuck his tongue out the corner of his mouth.

Shaking his head, Isaac rubbed his hands over his face and sat upright. Henley leaned forward, pressing a kiss to Isaac's mouth, and pulled away. "Boss said PDA's must be kept to a minimum but didn't say we couldn't do anything at all."

Isaac laughed. "Come on, sweetheart. Let's go home."

# CHAPTER
# TWELVE

## ISAAC

"Yeah, he's mine, so you can't have him," Henley stated as he strode over to Isaac and wrapped his arms around his waist.

"Henley!" Isaac admonished.

"She was asking!"

"You're also asking…" He left the rest of that sentence out, knowing exactly what conclusion Henley would come to.

Henley bit his lip, and Isaac knew he wanted to say, "Yes, Daddy," but wouldn't while they were working. Since Mr Sanders had confirmed their relationship was fine two weeks ago, Henley had been a lot more visibly flirtatious at work, and although Isaac didn't mind, he didn't want their work to suffer, or for the stores they were visiting to complain. Their boss hadn't named names for the claimant of the sexual harassment accusation, but he wanted to keep his head down, none-theless.

"Aww, that's so cute!" the brown-haired woman said, clasping her hands at her chest.

They worked through the sudden influx of staff before there was a break, and Isaac took the opportunity to talk to Henley about the following week.

"So, do you have any questions about next week? Anything you're unsure about?" Isaac carried the cups to Henley, setting Henley's tea in front of him and wrapping his hands around his coffee.

"What's next week?" Henley's brow furrowed.

"The end of your training. You'll be on your own from next week."

"I…You…" Henley ducked his head, appearing to be lost for words.

"You knew it was coming. You can't work with me all the time." Isaac sat down next to him, resting his hand on his back.

"I know. I just…it seems like it's gone so quickly." Henley smiled, a fake one if ever there was, and added, "But I'll be fine. I can't think of anything I may have problems with, and you're at the end of a phone if there is."

Isaac knew Henley was trying to sound cheerful, but he was failing abysmally.

"You will be absolutely fine, Henley. I have no worries about you at all." Except for his current reaction to working alone, which was concerning. As Isaac had told Henley, he knew it was coming, it was part of the job description that execs worked alone unless the store was a large one, when usually two execs worked together, but it didn't happen often.

Henley appeared more subdued for the rest of the day, and Isaac decided he needed to rest and relax when they got home. Luckily, Isaac had driven them both that day, so he could drive them home and allow Henley to work through whatever was bugging him. Although that was what he did, Isaac was unused to the quiet interior for the three-hour journey. It was funny how easy it was to get comfortable with a new normal.

There wasn't a murmur of protest from Henley when Isaac parked at his apartment. He exited the car, grabbed his bag and followed Isaac up. When they entered, Isaac did what he'd wanted to do all day, he began pampering his boy. He helped him out of his coat and shoes, took his bag from him, grabbed him a glass of juice and hustled him to the bathroom. Isaac was becoming concerned with how quiet Henley was.

Sitting Henley on the closed toilet seat, Isaac plugged the bath and turned on the taps. As he squirted in some muscle relaxing bubble bath, the scent of lavender filled the room.

Isaac noticed Henley had not drunk his juice. "Drink, sweetheart." He furrowed his brow at the vacant expression on Henley's face. Isaac made a decision. If Henley was not talking or responding by the time the bath was ready, he would call in reinforcements.

At his push, Henley drank the juice, a few sips before draining the whole glass. Isaac exhaled for the first time since entering the apartment. The whole Daddy lifestyle was different for each person, and although there were some similarities between relationships, most of it was fine-tuned for the specific boy. So, what worked for Mateo wouldn't necessarily be what Henley needed. It was Isaac's job to figure out the best way to take care of Henley, and if he needed help to do that, so be it.

When Henley had finished his juice, Isaac took the glass from him and pulled him up to stand. The buttons on his pale blue shirt were small, and Isaac fumbled a bit, but before long, they were undone. Sliding his hands up Henley's chest and over his shoulders, he pushed the shirt off and let it fall to the floor. Henley's gaze was now on Isaac, a little spark kindling in the blue depths.

Isaac glanced down, pulling the belt from its clasp and removing it from the belt loops before dropping it with the shirt. Gaze still on his hands, Isaac unfastened the trouser buttons and zipper, allowing them to drop to the floor. Henley was left in his briefs, which enclosed a semi-hard cock. Isaac raised an eyebrow. If Henley was only partially hard at this point, something was definitely weighing on his mind.

Seemingly without thought, Isaac's hands found their way into the waistband of Henley's underwear and pushed them under his ass, sliding his hands forward to lift it over his shaft. Inhaling and clenching his jaw to withhold from reaching for the beautiful sight, Isaac dropped to his knees...for a different reason. He tapped Henley's left foot, removing the layers of material and his sock, and repeated on the other side.

Once Henley was stripped, Isaac switched off the taps and grabbed Henley's hand, leading him to the soothing warmth. Helping him into the bath, Isaac crouched and propped a bath pillow behind his head.

"Rest, sweetheart. I will be back in a few minutes. Alright?" He brushed his hand across Henley's hair.

"Yes, Daddy," Henley mumbled, eyes closed.

"Don't fall asleep, though," Isaac whispered as he pressed a kiss to the side of his head.

A ghost of a smile formed on Henley's mouth, so Isaac called that a win. He exited the bathroom and strode to the front door, where he had left his coat and phone. Unlocking his phone, he called up a contact, dialled and pressed it to his ear.

"Hey, Isaac. Is everything alright?"

"I hope so, Ariel, but I need your help."

"Is Henley okay? What can I do?" She shushed someone—probably Arianne—on the other end of the line.

"He's…alright, but he's gone silent on me. I mentioned that next week he would be working by himself, and he withdrew into himself. I'm dealing with it as I would, but I wondered whether having his sisters, family or friends around him would be better? What do you think?"

"He certainly doesn't need to go out," she said in a motherly tone. "I think if you had a couple of people over to distract him, he might open up later on."

Isaac nodded, though she couldn't see him. "That's what I thought. Who is best, though? Sisters?"

"Yes. Arianne and I will come over, and I'll see if I can get Becca to come as well. Tracey is out of town, but we can always get her on video call if needed."

"Thanks, Ariel. I appreciate this."

"You're welcome, Isaac. You've been looking after him so well, let us take some of the burdens for now."

Isaac didn't mention that none of this was considered a burden as far as he was concerned, he wanted what was best for Henley, and he was still learning what that was. At this moment, Henley was unable to tell him what he wanted, so he had to go to another source.

He gave Ariel his address, and she promised to be there in an hour. It gave him enough time to get Henley cleaned and dressed in comfortable clothes.

He put a few snacks and another juice on a tray and took it to the sofa. When Henley was out, he'd sit down with him and feed him a few bites until his sisters arrived when he would order takeaway for them all.

The bathroom was overly warm when he returned, and he rolled up his sleeves before kneeling next to the bath.

"Hey, sweetheart. How are you feeling?"

"Like a limp noodle," came the response, causing Isaac to chuckle and his tension to release a little. If Henley was making jokes, he was coming back to earth.

"Perfect. Let's get you cleaned up." He reached for a sponge and the body wash, soaping it up and rubbing it across every inch of skin he could reach. Sliding his arm behind Henley and lifting him forward so he could wash his back, Isaac understood what Henley meant about being so relaxed. He was a lot heavier than usual, but he managed.

After cleaning and rinsing his back, Isaac helped him sit back again and brushed the sponge down his stomach to his groin. The soft cock perked up a little, but Isaac purposefully avoided that area, for now. He lifted each of Henley's legs then moved back up to his shaft. This time he grabbed Henley's cock to clean all around and under it and his balls, sliding the sponge into his crack, as well.

By the time he was finished, Henley's cock was happy to see him. Leaning back to check the clock through the open door, which was situated on the wall of the bedroom, he realised they had a bit of time.

Isaac grasped Henley's cock in a tight fist, stroking up and down in slow movements. As he reached the head, he added a twist of his hand, like he'd seen Henley do previously, before retracing his path. Henley's hips twitched in response to the stimulus, and his throaty moans were escalating. He increased his speed, and Henley's hands reached up to grasp the handles on the side of the bath, gripping them tightly.

"Please, Daddy. I'm so close." Henley's head thrashed on the pillow as the water rippled around his body in time with Henley's thrusts up into Isaac's hand.

"Come, sweet boy. Come for me."

Isaac watched the expressions crossing Henley's

face as the orgasm ripped through him. His mouth gaped open, and his back arched just before his climax hit, then his stomach contracted, and he curled in on himself as his cock released his come. Henley's eyes were squeezed shut, his breathing laboured, and a flush coated his body. Beads of perspiration slid down his cheeks as his arms dropped into the bath, and his head rested back.

Complete and utter relaxation. Mission accomplished.

Isaac smiled at Henley and stood to grab a towel from the radiator. "Come on, sleepyhead. Time to get out." Hooking the towel over his forearm, Isaac held out his hands for Henley's, taking his weight and pulling him to stand when he grabbed on. Once he had stepped out of the bath, Isaac quickly towelled him off and wrapped the towel around his waist.

Linking their fingers together, Isaac dragged Henley to the bedroom and sat him on the end of the bed. Turning to the drawers, he contemplated the options. Henley had brought a few clothes to keep here over the last couple of weeks, so he had a change of clothes if he needed them, so at least Isaac didn't have to find something of his own to fit him.

Choosing a tank, a fluffy jumper and some pyjama bottoms, Isaac pivoted back to Henley. He kneeled in front of him once more, gazing into his eyes.

"How do you feel, sweetheart?" he asked as he slid the pyjamas on, helping Henley to stand momentarily when he removed the towel and pulled up the trousers.

Henley sniffed as he sat. "Cared for." He lifted his gaze to Isaac's. "Loved," he whispered.

Isaac smiled and cupped his cheek. "You are."

Tears shimmered in Henley's eyes, but a beautiful grin lit up his face. There was his boy. Henley was coming back to him.

Isaac helped Henley into the tank and jumper and watched as Henley snuggled himself into it. He made a mental note that the jumper was a comfort for Henley. He might need that information in the future.

"I've got some snacks ready. Come on." Threading their fingers once more, Isaac led the way to the sofa, sitting and positioning Henley's side to his chest, Henley's back against the arm of the sofa. The tray was within reach, so he passed Henley the juice, encouraging him to drink it all, and picked up some grapes. One by one, he fed them to Henley, enjoying each time Henley took a piece from his hand and rested his head on Isaac's shoulder as he chewed it.

Once the food and juice were gone, Isaac pushed the tray away and wrapped his arms fully around Henley. They stayed that way until the doorbell rang. Henley lifted his head, his forehead creased.

"Who's that?"

Isaac smiled. "We won't know unless we open the door."

Henley chuckled and stood. Isaac helped steady him before shuffling in the direction of the door. He opened it with a flourish, beckoning everyone in when he saw Henley's three sisters. "Welcome, ladies."

"What are you girls doing here?" Henley gaped, a

slow smile spreading across his face as he saw Ariel, Arianne and Becca.

Ariel came forward and wrapped Henley in a hug. "A little bird told us we might be needed."

Isaac caught Henley's gaze over her shoulder, and Henley mouthed, "Thank you." Isaac waved it away.

"I thought we could order some takeaway. What's everyone's choice?" Isaac said, heading to the kitchen counter.

"Chinese!" Several voices shouted at once.

Isaac chuckled. "I think the answer might be Chinese. But each of you needs to be a little more specific." He finally managed to finagle their preferences and placed the order. "They said it should be around forty minutes."

"Perfect. Time for a pampering session, Henley!" Arianne clapped. "Your hair needs a little colour. What do you think, Isaac?"

"I think Henley can have whatever he wants."

"Ooh, keep him, Henley," Becca thumbed over her shoulder.

"I intend to."

"Right. I'll leave you to your hair discussion," Isaac said and wandered towards the hall.

"Wait!" Henley ran to Isaac and threw his arms around his neck. "Thank you! Thank you! Thank you!"

"You're welcome, sweetheart. Have fun. Later, we need to talk."

"I know. We will."

Isaac pressed a kiss to the centre of Henley's forehead, then on his lips before gently pushing him in his sisters' direction. "Enjoy."

Henley grinned and whirled around, sashaying his hips in an exaggerated sway as he moved back to his family. Isaac had no plans for what he would do, but he could listen to some music and read a book while they visited. It was nice to see Henley smiling again.

# CHAPTER THIRTEEN

## HENLEY

Henley was overwhelmed by how generous Isaac was. Not just with his money, but with his time. He knew Isaac wanted to spend time with him to talk him through his issues, but instead, Isaac gave him what he knew Henley needed to help him find his equilibrium again. His family.

His sisters stayed for a couple of hours, making sure his hair was perfectly coloured, and his nails were manicured. Isaac had only joined them when the food had arrived, then he'd retreated to the bedroom.

Henley now stood in the doorway to the bedroom, watching as Isaac nodded his head to whatever music was playing through the headphones. He was on his laptop, sitting with his back against the headboard and his legs stretched out. Henley knew Isaac was conscious of the weight he carried around his waist, but Henley loved it. And as for the rest of the package…Henley wouldn't be complaining. Ever.

His heart raced as he realised how much he hoped their relationship would last. He was falling for—had fallen for—this amazing person, and he didn't want to ever let him go.

Isaac noticed him, and his mouth curled as he pulled off the headphones. "Hey. Everything okay?"

"Yes. They've gone. They said to say goodbye."

"Did you have fun?" Isaac swung his legs off the bed, coming upright and pushed the laptop closed.

"It was amazing, thank you so much, Daddy!" Now that Isaac had hold of nothing that would break, Henley skipped across the room and flung his arms around Isaac as he had done earlier. "I can't believe you did that for me. Thank you."

"I would do anything for you, sweetheart. I told you right from the beginning that my job is to take care of you. I have your best interests at heart, and if it's something I can't give you myself, I will find someone who can. Tonight, you needed to unwind with your sisters." Isaac ruffled his hair. "I love the colour, by the way."

Henley pulled away and ran his hands through his hair. "It's your favourite colour."

"I know, but you didn't have to do that for me."

"I wanted it. I like blue a whole lot more now that I know you do."

Isaac snickered. "So long as you're happy with it, that's all that matters."

"Very happy."

Isaac rubbed a hand up and down Henley's back. "We need to talk. I know it's late, but it would be better to get this conversation done so we can start sorting it out."

"I know."

"Let's get ready for bed, and we'll snuggle up and talk it through, okay?"

"Yes, Daddy."

They went through their usual routine, Isaac helping Henley get ready as well as himself, and Isaac heading to the kitchen to grab them fresh drinks for overnight. It was something Isaac always did, but Henley had never thought about doing for himself.

When they were settled with Henley draped across Isaac's front, their legs and arms entwined, Isaac asked his first question.

"Can you tell me what happened earlier?"

Henley thought back to earlier in the day, although now, it seemed a lot longer ago. "I guess I forgot I would be working alone. I'm so used to working alongside you, it escaped my notice that it would soon be over."

"It's not over, Henley. I promise you."

"No, I don't mean us. I mean working together. I've had so much fun these last few weeks, I guess…I'm worried that I won't like the job as much if you're not there with me. And that I won't see you as much because of where we will be working."

Isaac was silent for a moment. "It's true we won't see as much of each other as we do now. There's nothing we can do about that, unfortunately. But we can figure out other stuff. Since we started our relationship, we have been together almost all day, every day. We've not spent a night apart." He hurried on before Henley could get lost in his head again, "And I love it. But the job demands some nights away. If that happens, we will sort out a routine for you to follow, we will be on the phone to each other or video calling. There are ways around it."

Henley considered Isaac's words. "It's not the same as when you're with me, though."

"No. It won't be the same. But we will manage because when we see each other again, it will be amazing. I'm not at all concerned about you being able to do the job. I know you can do it. You are fantastic with the staff and everything else that the job entails."

Henley preened under the praise. "I am good, aren't I?"

"And so modest, too." Isaac snorted then sobered. "If something happens and one of us is unhappy with how things are working, we will talk about it and find a solution. The only way this will work is if we communicate."

"Okay. I understand."

"Do you feel better about next week now?"

Henley smoothed his hand across Isaac's chest, above his heart. "I do. We just need to talk."

Isaac pressed a kiss to the top of his head and held him tighter.

"As we have a bit of time before we have to leave, you need to take your punishment," Isaac declared the following morning.

Henley spun around, eyes wide. "What! What did I do?"

Isaac raised his eyebrows. "Going silent on me yesterday. What did I tell you when we first started this relationship?"

"That you do what's in my best interests." Henley twisted his hands around each other and bit his lip.

"Yes, and what else?"

Henley studied the floor, trying to remember everything they had talked about. He could feel himself getting flustered because he couldn't remember.

"That you need to tell me the truth at all times, even when it scares you," Isaac answered his own question when Henley fumbled for a response. Henley ducked his head. Isaac's hand brought his chin back up. "I'm not cross with you. We talked it out last night and fixed it. But I would've preferred to sort it out immediately. You had me worried for a long while yesterday. You need to remember to trust me, trust us, trust in this." Isaac pointed from Henley to himself several times.

"Yes, Daddy. It's hard sometimes. I've been on my own for so long…"

"I know. But that's why I need to remind you." Isaac got a glimmer in his eye that Henley wasn't sure he could trust. He squinted at Isaac, trying to gauge what he was thinking as his stomach somersaulted. "Stand facing the wall, hands braced, legs apart."

Henley walked over to the wall on shaky legs and assumed the position. His breathing increased, and he could feel rivulets of sweat running down the side of his face.

"Good boy."

Isaac stood behind him. Henley could feel his presence. Isaac reached around to undo Henley's trousers, letting them fall to his knees, where his position prevented them from dropping to the floor. Isaac pulled his briefs out of the way in the same manner, leaving his ass bare to Isaac's roaming hands. He squeezed one cheek then the other before announcing, "Ready?"

"Yes, Daddy." He bit his lip to contain the sob that wanted to break free. He hated that he'd disappointed Isaac. That hurt worse than the pain of the spanking would, he was sure.

Isaac's hand left his skin and returned with a short, sharp smack on the fleshy part of his ass. Henley grimaced at the sting, holding his breath until the pain reduced. The second smack smarted his other cheek, and he clenched his ass and thrust forward, away from the pain. As he settled back into his original position, a third slap caught his lower buttock and upper thigh, quickly followed by a fourth on the opposite side. Henley blinked back tears and gritted his teeth as Isaac smoothed his hands across the sensitive skin.

When Isaac's hand left his ass, Henley braced for

more. Locking his knees as the next threatened to take him down, Henley's tears cascaded down his face. He swallowed against the lump in his throat, knowing this spanking *was* a punishment rather than pleasure. He had scared his Daddy, and his Daddy needed to remind him.

Henley rested his head against the wall, writhing in place with every stinging smack, but knowing it was for the best. A sob left him, although he tried to stifle it.

Isaac's hands smoothed across his undoubtedly reddened skin, the sensitivity making it feel like pins were sticking in him. "Good boy. Such a good boy for your Daddy," he whispered in Henley's ear as he wrapped his arms around him from behind. Henley turned, wanting the full embrace, and he snuggled his face into Isaac's neck and cried.

"I'm sorry, Daddy. I'm sorry," he repeated.

Isaac stroked his hair and back until Henley calmed. Taking a large inhale and a cathartic exhale, Henley lifted his head. He felt rejuvenated, which he hadn't expected.

"All is forgiven, sweetheart. Done and dusted. Well done, sweet boy."

"Thank you, Daddy."

A sense of calm and pride flowed through him.

"Turn back to the wall for a minute. I want to put some lotion on you," Isaac said.

Henley obeyed as he always would, and the cold cream made him jump before soothing his ass as it was rubbed into his sensitive skin.

"All done. Let's get to work. We're running a little

behind schedule now." Isaac reached down and pulled Henley's briefs back over his ass and did the same with his trousers.

The material rubbed annoyingly against his ass, and he knew it would be a hundred times worse when he sat in the car. Henley grabbed the things he needed for the day, and they headed out. As he'd predicted, his ass felt like it was on fire as soon as he was seated, but he breathed through the pain, remembering the lesson he was being taught.

It was remembering the lesson that gave Henley the courage to ask Isaac for something he'd been thinking about for a while.

"Daddy?"

"Yes, sweetheart."

"Would you…Will you…" He breathed deeply and started again, "I'd like you to meet Dad and Pops."

"Sure. Whenever you want me to."

No shock. No horror. No denying him. Just, "Sure." A weight lifted off his shoulders that he never realised was there. He'd wanted to ask for a while but had thought it was too soon. Although Isaac had met all but one of his sisters now.

"Thank you. I'll speak to them and ask."

"Perfect. You can meet my family whenever you would like to. We have a Friday family dinner, which, as you know, is why early evenings on Fridays is always a tricky time for me. You are more than welcome to meet them as soon as you are ready."

Henley thought about this. He wanted to know

what his dads thought first. "Maybe after you've met mine?"

"Okay."

Henley had an idea. "I think we should join our work nights out together." Henley had been going out once with the execs and once with the customer service staff. It made sense, at least to him, that they should join forces. More people, more fun.

Isaac's forehead creased, his brows knitting in the middle. "I'm not sure. We usually get together at the Christmas party or some other company celebration, but I don't know if the departments will mix well."

"Could we ask them and try?"

Isaac's face cleared as he smiled. "We can ask. The worst they can say is no."

"Yay!" Henley clapped his hands together, wincing when his fidgeting caused his ass to burn.

"You okay?" Isaac asked, glancing over.

"Yeah. I'm fine."

Their journey was a short one that day, only an hour away, and soon they were busy with boxes, clothing, orders and complaints. Henley loved every minute of it. When he first applied for it, he knew he would be able to do the job, but he didn't realise how much he would enjoy meeting new people each day. Even travelling, although tedious some days, was fun. However, maybe that was because he had been with Isaac for most of it.

He knew the following week—four more days— would be his first visit to a store alone. Despite being anxious about not seeing Isaac as much, Henley was looking forward to the actual work.

At lunchtime, he saw he'd received a text from Tracey, so he decided to call her and see if he could catch her before she was busy again.

"Hey! I got your message. How are you doing, stranger?" he said with a grin.

"You can talk, Mr I've-got-a-new-guy," she countered.

"Oi! I see you all!"

"Not as much as you did."

"And I bet you're glad about that!" He giggled.

"Too right, troublemaker."

"Anyway, how are you?" Henley was worried about Tracey. She had been more distant than usual over the last few weeks, missing more of their family time than ever before.

"I'm alright." Henley heard her sigh. "I've taken a new job, but I haven't told Dad and Pops yet."

"Why not? You're not a call girl, are you?"

"What! No, you asswipe! Jeez! I'm a PA still, but it's for a larger company, and I'm the first port of call for the owner. He travels a lot; hence, I do now. It's a twenty-four-hour day thing. I don't want Dad and Pops worrying about me working too hard."

Henley understood the undertones of what she was trying to say. Dad and Pops, while they meant well, if they get a bugbear about something they thought was harming their children, there was no stopping them. If they believed Tracey's new job was too much for her, they would go on and on at her about it. They wanted the best for them, but they don't like their children doing more than they needed to.

"Congrats. It sounds like a good job. You always wanted to travel, now you get to do that. But be careful, please, Trace. I love you, and I don't want you working yourself to the bone for this guy."

"I love you, too. And I will be careful. I will also do everything in my power to be fan-fucking-tastic at this job because I love it."

Henley laughed. "Good. Anyway, loser, some of us have to work. I'll catch you later, gator."

"See ya, Hen."

Though their conversation was short, it was bittersweet. Henley often thought Tracey pictured herself as an outsider because she was brought into their family when she was older, but none of the other family members thought of her that way. Every one of them tried to show her she was perfect for their family. Unfortunately, her gremlins got in the way sometimes.

Henley switched off his phone and shook his head.

"You're worried about her, aren't you?" Isaac said, coming to crouch next to Henley's chair.

Nodding slowly, Henley gave a lopsided grin. "She works too hard, but she loves it. Who am I to complain?"

"You're not complaining, you're worried and have every right to be. She's your sister." Isaac rubbed Henley's back soothingly. "I set Sarah up on a date with a guy from a café we went to once. I didn't know him but when I spoke to him, I trusted my instincts and got him to take her out. They're getting on well, but I still worry about her. Same for Felicity. Doesn't matter what age they are, you will always worry about family. Nothing you can do apart from loving and supporting her."

Isaac was right, as usual.

# CHAPTER FOURTEEN

## ISAAC

Henley had been working alone for the past three weeks. Every time they spoke on the phone, Isaac could tell he was having a good day and was excited about what he was doing. He could also hear the melancholy of not having Isaac with him.

As Isaac had predicted, Henley came to Isaac's house any night they were both at home. They had only been apart four nights.

It was because of this that Isaac decided to change things. Or, at least, to ask Henley an important question, despite having only been together for a short time, Isaac knew it was the right decision.

He had been to Henley's parents' house the week before, and they had welcomed him with open arms. Isaac had decided there and then, he needed Henley in his life for as long as he could have him.

*Pops, as he asked Isaac to call him, cornered him in the hallway after dinner. Isaac could tell something was on his mind, and he was happy to listen and talk through anything they needed. He would do anything for Henley.*

*"Henley is incredibly special, Isaac. You need to treat him with care and consideration, especially with the age difference. I'm not saying I disagree with it because I don't, but please be careful with him. He's a soft soul."*

*"I know he is, and he's precious to me. I would like to ask him to move in with me. He's been struggling with our work schedule, and I think having a place that is ours to come home to each time, even when I can't be there, would be helpful to him. Do you agree?"*

*He hadn't planned on asking Pops for his advice, but the words just came out.*

*"Don't you think that's a little soon?"*

*"Not really. We spend so much of our time together already. If something is going to go wrong in our relationship, it would more than likely happen once we're living together. God forbid, but if that happens, why not figure it out sooner rather than later?"*

*Pops paused, gaze roaming Isaac's face. "I think that's an incredibly good idea. I like that you take care of him, Isaac."*

*"It's who I am," Isaac replied.*

After that, they did not mention it again, but he could see a new light shining in Pops' eyes, and he was happy he'd been able to give Henley's parents some peace of mind.

So, tonight, he was planning on asking Henley to move in, officially. Henley already had a key, but Isaac wanted to do it properly. If he ever got home. Henley had rung from the road saying the traffic was awful because of an accident on the motorway, and with it being Friday as well, tailbacks were miles long. Isaac had been keeping an eye on the travel news and traffic reports. He'd not heard from Henley in over half an hour, though, so he tried calling him. No answer.

He began pacing the floor, worry flooding his body until a key turned in the latch. He whirled towards the door, seeing a haggard, tired-looking Henley entering. Isaac hustled over to him and wrapped him in his arms, squeezing him tight.

"I missed you, Daddy," Henley said, voice strained.

"I missed you, too, sweetheart."

They stayed in the embrace for several long minutes, Isaac breathing in Henley's scent, reaffirming he was there and safe. Isaac pulled back, cupping Henley's face and pressing their lips together in a sweet kiss.

"Dinner is ready. I just need to warm it up. Are you ready for it now?"

"Yes, please, Daddy. I'm starving!"

"I thought you might be." Isaac leaned down to help Henley with his shoes, led him to the breakfast bar and sat him down with a brief kiss. Isaac filled a glass with juice and placed it in front of Henley. "Drink up while I warm your food. Tell me about your day."

Henley's voice was excited as he spoke about the store he'd visited that day. He and the manager got on well together, which was great news. A good rapport with managers always went a long way to building good relationships.

When Henley's food was ready, Isaac gave it to him and sat next to him at the counter. In between bites, Henley continued his story. Once he had finished, Henley appeared to wilt.

"You're worn out."

"I'm so glad it's Friday. I love the job, but god!"

Isaac chuckled. "Well, I have something I want to talk to you about." Henley looked at him, and Isaac could see the worry creeping into his eyes. "Nothing bad." He twisted on the stool to face Henley and took his hands in his. "As my mother would say, this may be locking the stable door after the horse has bolted, but I would like you to consider moving in with me."

Henley gaped, mouth opening and closing. Isaac gave him a moment for the idea to sink in before saying any more.

"Seriously?"

For once, there wasn't much of an expression on Henley's face, apart from surprise. "Yes. I'd like you to move in."

"Move in here?"

Isaac nodded, trying not to feel uneasy with how long it was taking Henley to give him an answer.

"Hell, yes!" Henley shouted as he jumped up and wrapped his arms around Isaac's neck.

Isaac's breath came easier, knowing Henley wanted this. "If you'd prefer, we can move to your house instead? I don't want you to feel like you have to live here because I asked."

"No! I love it here. This apartment feels more like home than my house does. Don't get me wrong, I've done what I could with it, but we've made so many memories here." Henley surveyed the apartment, arms loosely encircling his neck.

Henley was right. Although they had spent time at Henley's house, most of their time had been here. "You could rent out your house. It would give you a bit more income on top of your wages." He knew the house meant a lot to Henley, too. Isaac didn't want Henley to get rid of it unless he had no other choice. And in the unlikely event, they didn't work out, Henley would still have the house. Isaac refused to take away his independence.

"When can I move in?" Henley beamed as he asked.

"Well…funnily enough, we don't have any plans this weekend, for once. No Friday night family dinner, no Saturday work night out, no Sunday family time. We have a whole two days, all to ourselves."

"But wouldn't you prefer using that time to do something we want to do instead of moving my stuff."

"There is nothing I would love better than making sure my boy knows his home is right here. And if that means we move your things in, we move your things in."

Henley bit his lip as his gaze roamed Isaac's face. "How about…we grab some people to help move me tomorrow and use Sunday as a rest day?"

"I think that sounds like a good plan, sweet boy. Tonight, however, I think you need to be rewarded."

Henley's gaze lit up. "You have worked so hard this week. I am so proud of you, Henley." Isaac slid his hand up Henley's spine to cradle the back of his head before taking his mouth in a hard, desperate kiss. Isaac wanted to reaffirm to himself that Henley was home, safe and *his*. But first, he needed to take care of his boy.

With one hand on the back of Henley's thigh, he pulled Henley's leg to his waist before running his other hand down to do the same for the other leg. Once Henley was off-balance, Isaac picked him up and sat him on the breakfast bar, lips never leaving each other.

Isaac unfastened Henley's trousers, pulling his shirt free and unbuttoning it enough for him to pull it over Henley's head. His lips went to Henley's jaw, down the column of his neck to his chest. Once there, he painted it with his tongue, circling his nipples as Henley gripped the back of Isaac's head.

"Brace your hands behind you," Isaac instructed, and as Henley did, Isaac yanked his trousers and briefs off in one go, quickly shucking the socks, too. The apartment was nice and warm, so he was not concerned with Henley getting cold. "Keep your hands there."

"Yes, Daddy," Henley moaned.

Isaac returned to kissing Henley's chest, and after some more teasing finally flicked his tongue over the nubs, he alternated between licking and sucking until Henley's hips were thrusting up into the air with nothing to gain friction against.

Still fully dressed apart from his jacket and tie, Isaac made sure to keep his body away from Henley. This was for Henley to relax, which he would do once he had climaxed.

Isaac nibbled his way down Henley's abs, licking along the defined muscles until he reached his destination, which was rising to meet him with an angry looking head.

"Please, Daddy."

Isaac could see Henley's hands clawing at the counter, knuckles white, and as Isaac blew across the top of his cock, Henley's arms failed him, and he dropped back to his elbows. Smiling, Isaac locked gazes with Henley and lapped up the precome seeping from the tip.

"Oh god! Oh god!" Henley chanted, his chest heaving with the force of his breaths.

Isaac wrapped his lips around Henley's shaft, flicking his tongue against the head and sank Henley's cock into his mouth. Isaac's hands had been sliding across every expanse of skin he could reach until he used one to push Henley's legs wider and the other to fondle his balls, pulling and rolling them in his palm.

Henley called out his name and thrust his hips upwards as Isaac's tongue found the sensitive area on the underside of his cock. Isaac slid a finger into his mouth and found Henley's hole. He rubbed a circle around it when he sucked Henley's cock down into his throat, and Henley's hips thrust up once more.

"Please, Daddy. I'm not going to last! Please!"

Henley panted with the effort of holding back, so Isaac decided to let him have this. He pulled off briefly.

"Come!" he commanded, swallowing Henley's cock as soon as the words were free.

"Fuck! Oh shit!"

Henley's spine hit the counter, and his hands went over his head to grip the edge of the bar as his orgasm hit. His feet were curled on a stool either side of Isaac's body. Isaac drank him down, the slightly bitter taste, not unpleasant but not strawberries and cream either.

When Henley's body became completely boneless where he lay, Isaac pulled off, earning a whimper and a twitch from Henley. He slid his hands over Henley's exposed body, calming, soothing, relaxing.

"I can't move," mumbled Henley.

Isaac chuckled and slid a hand under Henley's back, lifting him to a seated position, or at least he tried to, but Henley was like a ragdoll. He rested Henley forward against his chest and wrapped his hands under his thighs to lift him. He stumbled to the bedroom—their bedroom—lying Henley on the already turned down bed.

"Rest, sweetheart. You've had a long week."

Henley snored in response, and, snickering, Isaac pulled the covers over him.

When he entered the kitchen, he picked his phone up and dialled.

"Hi. He's agreed to move in. Would you mind asking his sisters if they could help us pack up his house tomorrow."

"Of course, I can. All four are here tonight, so that

works well." Pops paused. "Ariel, I will tell you in a minute. Be patient, girl. Sorry about that. Yes, I'm sure it won't be a problem. Lewis and I will be there, too, even if we just direct everyone."

"Perfect, thanks. I'm going to call in some more reinforcements as well. The quicker we get it done, the quicker everyone can have their weekend free."

"See you tomorrow."

"Bye, Pops."

He cancelled the call and made another.

"Hey, Blake. Are you busy tomorrow by any chance?"

"Not at all. What do you need?"

"Henley's moving in. We need some assistance to get it done quickly."

"No problem, text me his address, and I'll be there."

"I'm ringing the rest of them, too. I want him in here asap."

Blake laughed. "Knew you'd be a goner when you found someone."

"What can I say?" Isaac laughed.

"Tell you what, you call Frankie, Jo and Sierra, I'll call the others. I'll text you with who's free."

"Thanks, Blake."

"No problem."

They rang off. Isaac reached for Henley's phone. Pulling up the contacts, he dialled.

"Henley! Nice to hear from you!"

"Sorry, Anne. It's Isaac."

"What's wrong? Is Henley okay?" Her voice was panicked.

"Yes, yes! He's fine. Sorry, I didn't mean to scare you. I was calling to ask for a favour." He explained yet again what he needed, and Anne agreed to help. Her twin sons were home from university, so she would get them to help, too. She also said she'd call Bernie and Neil.

For the final time, he dialled from his phone. "Hey, Dad. I'm calling in the cavalry."

"What did you do?"

Isaac laughed. "I didn't do anything. Henley's moving in. We need some muscle tomorrow to get it done. I've got a fair number of people already, but I wondered if you could ask around who of the family is free and send them over tomorrow."

"Of course, I can."

"I'll text you Henley's address. Thanks, Dad."

"You're welcome, son. It will be nice to meet him finally."

They said their goodbyes, and Isaac blew out a breath. If he counted correctly, and everyone he'd called was able to come, there should be approximately thirty people helping. He wasn't joking when he said he wanted it done quickly. He didn't want Henley to have the chance to change his mind, although if he did, Isaac wouldn't argue; he would ensure everything was returned to where Henley wanted it and back away slowly.

Isaac also wanted it done quickly so they would have more time together. It wasn't often their weekends were this empty, which, although it was a shame they had chosen to do it this weekend, it was the best weekend to do it.

Soon, he would have Henley to come home to or to have Henley come home to him. He couldn't wait to take care of his boy, twenty-four-seven.

# CHAPTER FIFTEEN

## HENLEY

Looking around the apartment—his home— Henley saw a mess, not to put too fine a point on it. Boxes were everywhere, the dining table couldn't be seen from the amount of stuff that was on it, and there were paths created between boxes so they could get from one area to the other. Despite that, though, Henley beamed.

He had decided to leave a lot of the furniture at the house, apart from the things he didn't want damaged. They were safely ensconced in the spare room at Isaac's apartment. The rest of the furniture would stay at the house so he could rent it out as part-furnished, gaining a higher income, at least in theory.

When Isaac and he had pulled up outside his house that morning, Henley had been overwhelmed with how busy it was. He'd never seen so many cars and people milling around. But they had all been fantastic, and the place had been cleared in next to no time. As a thank you, Henley ordered a variety of food from different places, so everyone had a choice of something for lunch. Becca had also baked up a storm with cookies and biscuits to tend to those with a sweet tooth.

As the afternoon had drawn on, Henley had watched their families interact with each other and their friends, and he was reminded of his idea of mixing the work nights. He'd spoken to Anne about it, and she'd been up for it. She said she'd bring her sons, too, which made Henley laugh. Her two sons had their eye on his twin sisters if he wasn't mistaken. Good luck to them.

Henley sighed as arms drew around his waist and pulled him closer to a warm, solid body.

"Having second thoughts?"

"No! Not at all. I was thinking about how everyone helped today. They were amazing."

"That they were." Isaac nuzzled his nose against Henley's neck, and Henley tilted his head to the side. "You smell delicious."

Henley laughed. "I'm sure sweat smells divine," he deadpanned.

"On you, it does." Isaac licked a strip up the column of Henley's neck, enclosing his earlobe in his lips and tugging. "You're mine, now, sweet boy," he whispered.

"Yours. Always and forever."

"I like the sound of that," Isaac growled, the sound sending tingles down Henley's spine and tenting his shorts.

Henley smoothed his hands along Isaac's forearms, which were still banded around him, protecting him, loving him. "I love you, Isaac." It was the first time he'd said it, but he knew it was true weeks ago.

Isaac stilled and rested his chin against Henley's shoulder. "I love you, too, sweetheart."

As soon as the words were spoken, Isaac spun him around and devoured him. One hand cupped his jaw, the other his ass, pulling him as close as possible, rocking their hips together.

Henley slid his hands to the hem of Isaac's t-shirt and underneath, pushing it up his body as his hands rose. When it was bunched under Isaac's armpits, Henley pulled away to yank it over his head before rejoining their mouths. Henley did the same with his own, causing Isaac to growl when he lifted his head once more. With a grin, Henley dived back in, wanting to give Isaac everything he could.

The sensation of their chests rubbing against each other, Isaac's light dusting of hair abrading Henley's skin deliciously, had Henley swaying so he could feel it more.

Isaac's hand found Henley's waistband and tugged the trousers off his hips. He kicked them free and found himself being walked backwards. Henley held on tight, knowing that, although there were boxes everywhere, Isaac would keep him safe from injury. When his ass rested against the sofa, he linked his hands at the back of Isaac's neck and concentrated on their kiss. Isaac's lips were perfection, giving and taking in equal measure. His tongue explored every part of Henley's mouth, leaving no area untouched.

As he became lightheaded, Henley lifted his head to break the seal, and Isaac kissed down his neck. Henley's cock was rock hard, as was Isaac's, so he reached for Isaac's trousers, attempting to remove them, but Isaac pushed his hands away and turned him to face the sofa.

Isaac pressed his covered cock into the valley between Henley's ass cheeks and held him upright and still. As much as Henley wanted to thrust against the sofa, Isaac held him tight.

"You're mine, Henley."

"Yours," Henley breathed.

Isaac bit his earlobe and released him, pushing against his upper back until he was leaning over the back of the sofa, his hands resting on the cushions. Hands grazed over his back, blunt nails causing goosebumps to follow in their wake. When they reached Henley's briefs, Isaac peeled them over his ass, pressing a kiss to each cheek before pulling them off completely.

Henley gasped as the fabric of the sofa chafed against his cock and the front of his thighs, but seconds later, he didn't care. Isaac's hands were back on his ass, kneading and spreading him while Isaac nibbled at his skin and licked it better. He heard Isaac spit, and his mouth was on his hole, licking, pressing, sucking, kissing repeatedly until Henley's mind was fuzzy from the pleasure. The sofa no longer scraped him, or if it did, he couldn't feel it.

All his senses were focused on that one part of him that was being teased beyond anything he'd ever felt before.

Hands and lips left him bereft, and he whimpered, pressing back for more, but when he heard the click of a cap, he settled, knowing Isaac would be back. A hand slid across his ass, spreading him again, and Henley stuck his ass out further. The cool gel made him jump when it was applied to his hole, but he soon didn't care. With Isaac's finger probing and finding entry, Henley was up in the clouds.

He lost all sense of time, only coming back to himself when he heard the rip of a wrapper and the click of the tube once more. The press of Isaac's cock against his hole had Henley gasping and pressing back. He wanted more. He wanted it all.

Words tumbled out of him. He had no idea what he was saying, but Isaac's hands rubbed up and down his back in a soothing gesture. Henley fell to his fore-arms, changing the position and allowing Isaac to slip further inside him. Henley wanted more. Pressing with his hands, he moved back, allowing Isaac to slide completely in.

"Fuck, Henley."

"Please!" Henley tried to move, but he was pinned between Isaac and the sofa. "Please, Daddy! Move, please!"

"I'll take care of you, sweetheart. Don't you worry, boy." Isaac withdrew and slammed back in, the screech of the sofa moving on the wooden floor echoing loudly. Neither cared because Isaac continued to thrust his hips in a quick, deep rhythm, holding tight to Henley's hips.

Henley received plenty of friction to his cock, and he was on the verge of coming, trying to pull back because his Daddy hadn't permitted him to come.

"Daddy! Please!"

Isaac reached under Henley's chest and pulled him upright, the change in position a relief on his cock but an explosion on his prostate. Henley reached his hands back, touching whatever skin he could reach of Isaac as he continued to pound into him, tweaking his nipples at the same time.

"Oh, fuck! Daddy! I'm going to come! Please!"

Isaac growled as he swore, and his cock emptied into Henley, his rhythm stuttering. "Come, Henley."

As soon as the words were spoken, Henley obeyed. No hands required. He rested his head back on Isaac's shoulder as the spasms flowed through him, and his cock released. Isaac caught him when his knees finally gave out, swinging him up into his arms and carrying him out of the room.

Henley wrapped his arms around Isaac's neck and rested his head on his shoulder again, content to be carried anywhere Isaac deemed necessary. Which happened to be the shower.

Isaac slid Henley down, keeping tight hold until he was certain Henley's legs would keep him upright, then reached to switch the shower on. Isaac kept his arms around Henley, smoothing his hands over his sweat-soaked skin, until the shower was ready, and helped Henley in, following straight after.

"I'm going to be asleep after this," Henley groused.

"Fine by me." Isaac yawned.

Henley snorted and burrowed further into Isaac's chest.

"We can sort everything out tomorrow." Isaac paused. "Although I will need to clean up the sofa. Either that or get it replaced."

Henley sniggered. "Sorry, Daddy."

"Don't need to be sorry, sweetheart. However, we can't go buying a new sofa every time that happens. It might be worthwhile getting a leather one or something."

Henley dropped his head back, staring up at his Daddy. "You're amazing," he sighed. Never had he felt more relaxed and content as he did at that moment.

Once they were in bed, the stain mopped up as best as they could, Henley snuggled into his favourite position.

"I love your family. They seemed to fit perfectly with mine, too. I never expected that."

"Why not?" Isaac slid his fingertips up and down his arm.

"Because we're so different. But maybe there's something to this nature versus nurture debate everyone talks about."

"As far as I'm concerned, our families got on. That's a win. End of." Isaac laughed.

"Yeah, I suppose there are plenty of people out there who hate their partner's family." Henley thought about everyone who turned up to help. He had been surprised to see the people from work—both departments. Henley hadn't expected them to work together. What with everything Isaac said about them not mixing well. "I think we should reconsider that dual night out, you know. Both departments worked well together today."

"Hmm." Isaac's tone was non-committal.

"At least let's ask the execs if they're interested. If they say no, fine. But we won't know until we ask."

"Alright, alright. We'll see what they say. But if they say no, you need to leave it alone," commanded Isaac.

"Yes, Daddy. I promise."

⟵——————⟶

Several weeks later, Henley looked around the bar, seeing the execs and customer service department mingling quite nicely together. He gave himself a mental pat on the back.

"You look far too smug," Isaac said, sliding his hand around Henley's shoulders and handing him a drink.

"I think I did good, don't you?" Henley ducked his head but peered up at Isaac through his eyelashes.

"You're a brat."

"I am not!"

"Yes, you are. You suckered me in by being sweet and obedient, and after moving in, you began pouting and doing things you knew you shouldn't." Isaac raised his eyebrows as he stared back at Henley.

"I was too close to the edge! I couldn't hold it in! If

I had so much as tried to put my trousers on, I would've come anyway. I thought it better to make sure my trousers stayed clean."

"Exactly. A brat." Isaac sipped his drink. "Which is why you're now wearing that." He nodded his head towards Henley's groin.

Henley had not been happy when Isaac's punishment had been a cock cage. He'd never worn one before, and he certainly wasn't planning on wearing one again. Which meant the punishment had worked as a deterrent. Isaac would be so pleased. Henley snorted.

"What?"

"I was thinking about how you'd be happy because the cage has worked as a punishment. I hate wearing it."

"Good. Maybe you will listen next time when I say…" Isaac leaned in, his mouth resting by Henley's ear as he growled, "your cock and orgasms belong to me."

Henley shivered as pleasure streamed through him, unable to go anywhere. He closed his eyes, cleared his throat and breathed deeply before refocusing on Isaac.

"They do seem to be getting along, though."

"It's because of you," Isaac stated bluntly.

Henley turned to him, brows lowered. "Me?"

Isaac nodded, gaze on their friends.

"What did I do?"

Isaac turned his body to face Henley and cupped his jaw. "You're the glue that brings us together. Without you, this merging would not have happened.

You bridged two departments and refused to sever ties —which is a good thing, by the way—therefore, bringing both together. No one else has done that. If anyone left customer service for execs, they cut away from their previous colleagues." Isaac pressed a chaste kiss to Henley's lips. "I'm so damn proud of you."

Henley loved hearing praise from his Daddy, but this was extra-special. His eyes flooded with tears, which soon rolled down his cheeks to be captured by Isaac's mouth and thumbs. His throat was too thick to say a word, so he clawed his arms around Isaac's body and held him tightly while he cried. It was a happy cry, so when someone came over to ask if he was okay, Isaac sent them away with a nod.

Hands and soothing words brought him back to himself however long later. Henley lifted his head, and a napkin was pressed in his hand, which he used to wipe his face. He couldn't see the state of Isaac's shirt, but he assumed it was tear and snot stained. Nice badge there.

"You okay, Henley?" Anne called from across the table, her forehead creased in concern.

"Yes. I'm fine." He indicated his face. "Happy tears." He chuckled.

Anne smiled. "Glad to hear it."

Isaac tucked Henley against him once more, passed him his drink, crossed his legs and started a conversation with Anne. As Henley looked around, he thought about bringing his sisters, and maybe Isaac's sisters, in on these nights out, too. What a hoot that would be. He could imagine the chaos. Although, Ariel and

Arianne had been seeing Anne's sons for the last couple of weeks, so he never knew if those guys would be tagging along as well. At the rate they were going, they'd need to book the whole bar themselves. Now, that's an idea. He smiled into his drink.

"I can hear the cogs working in your brain. What are you up to now?" Isaac groused into his ear.

"Nothing," Henley replied as innocently as he could. They both knew better, but Henley couldn't resist denying it.

"As I said. Brat."

Henley snorted and burst into laughter when Anne joined him, Isaac following not long after.

# EIGHTEEN MONTHS LATER

## ISAAC

He lifted the beer bottle to his mouth, gaze on Henley as he raced around the garden with his sisters. With how they acted when they were together, anyone would have thought they were kids if their actual height and age were taken out of the equation. Arial and Arianne chased after Henley with water guns, spraying far and wide, but luckily far enough away from the food for it not to matter. Several guests might not like it, but they were welcome to move away from the shenanigans.

As far as he was concerned, the joy on their faces was more than enough to counter anything else.

"Isaac!"

He turned to Pops, who was beckoning him over with his head. Isaac stood and ambled over to the older man.

"You okay, Pops?" He crouched down beside his chair, resting his hand on the much frailer arm. A stroke, eight months ago, had taken Pops down for a short while. Everyone had been shocked that the strong, confident, and yes, grumpy man had been knocked down by the silent attack. Luckily, Becca had been there and dealt with it quickly, although she was understandably shaken by it.

"Yes, son. Taking it easy, you know how it goes." Pops smiled, the left side of his face remaining expressionless. "Can you help Lewis, please. He says he's fine, but you know what he's like."

"Of course, I can, Pops. You stay here and keep an eye on my beer, alright?" Isaac winked at him and stood, stepping over to the barbecue where Lewis was wielding the tongs. "Hey, Dad. Why don't you go sit in the shade with your other half and give me a whirl on this beauty?"

Lewis nodded and drifted over to his husband. When Lewis had told him about and shown him the barbecue, Isaac had been impressed by the size the James family had. Lewis had explained that with five kids and several friends over, they had needed it. Isaac had scoffed at the time, but when everyone had arrived today, he'd understood what Lewis had meant.

The number of people in attendance was astounding, and the reason was nothing more than they had been invited to a barbecue. Simply good food and good company. There was no celebration or anything.

Well, until later, anyway. Isaac smirked and peered

at the food over the hot coals. He had a few minutes before things needed to be done, so his gaze wandered around the vast garden, finding his gorgeous boyfriend.

Today, Henley had gone all out with his outfit. With it being a sunny day, he was wearing a white tank covered with rainbow sequins in random patterns, purple skinny jeans with a black stud belt and silver ballet flats. The outfit was completed with his usual bangles, chain, earrings, rings and the rainbow keyring attached to his belt hoops. All in all, he was mesmerising, and that had nothing to do with the continual flicker of light coming from the reflection on his sequins.

Isaac shook his head and shouted to let guests know the food was ready. Once everyone had something and had found somewhere to sit, Isaac grabbed his own and found a place next to a slightly wet Henley.

"Hey," Henley said, eyes lighting up at seeing Isaac, something he would never get tired of witnessing. Henley leaned to the side for a kiss, which Isaac would never refuse. He tasted of beer, cheese and ketchup.

They leisurely kissed, sipping at each other's lips as Isaac held Henley's chin in place until catcalls and whistles broke them apart with a laugh.

Isaac wrapped his arm around Henley's shoulder, feeling more content than he had in an awfully long time. A few butterflies took flight in his stomach as he thought forward to his surprise for Henley. Nobody knew about it. Absolutely nobody. Isaac had hoped he'd read their situation correctly; otherwise, he was in for a disheartening evening. He needed to keep it together for another hour.

They mingled after the food, Becca taking over the grill. Isaac had been to Henley's parents' place so many times over the last year or so that he knew everyone now. But Henley enjoyed speaking to all the people visiting them. When Isaac had asked several months ago why Henley needed to speak to everyone every time he saw them, Henley replied, "You never know when it will be the last time you'll see that person, so what does it matter if I spend five seconds saying hello if it brightens their day a little." Isaac hadn't been complaining, simply curious, but Henley's explanation had stayed with him. It was so true, and such a simple thing that could mean a lot to someone else.

Henley had a heart of gold, and everyone knew it. Unfortunately, it also meant he could be taken advantage of. Several months after he started working alone as an exec, Henley had come home looking worn out after several days away. He and Leon had been opening a store in Scotland, and as soon as he'd walked through their front door, Isaac knew something was wrong.

When Isaac finally pried every piece of information from Henley that he could, he was furious. Leon hadn't lifted a finger to do anything the whole time they were there. He had left it all on Henley, and if there were complaints, Leon pointed to Henley as being incompetent. Isaac had immediately called Mr Sanders and explained the situation, demanding Leon's immediate dismissal.

Henley had been dealing with harassment for months and hadn't told Isaac, thinking he wouldn't be believed. Leon was particularly good at misdirecting people. Isaac had seen several things on their nights out—mainly Leon's disrespect for the LGBTQ+ community—and had challenged it. But once he'd turned that onto Henley, all bets were off.

That same night, Isaac had pampered and taken care of Henley enough to make up for feeling like a failure. Isaac should've seen what was happening but hadn't. Two days later, he'd finally reconciled everything in his head, and Henley had been punished for keeping it a secret. Henley had been doing so well with communicating between them, but this was too much. Months of secrets agonised Isaac, and he couldn't deal with Henley doing that again. So, he'd punished Henley as he had done at the beginning of their relationship, but poor Henley hadn't been allowed to come for three days—a lifetime in Henley's world.

Isaac returned to the present when the bell sounded. As was routine at these get-togethers now, when the bell rang, everyone had to make a circle—or as best a circle as they could depending on how many were there—and tell everyone something good that happened to them since they had last visited. At first, Isaac had been unsure what to say, because his happiness was so wrapped up in Henley, but with Henley's help, he'd been able to see outside the box.

This time, though, things would be different.

Becca and Ariel helped Pops down the steps to a chair placed in the circle next to Lewis. They both sat on their 'thrones' as the guests gathered around them.

Lewis began, "This is what family is all about. It doesn't have to be about blood. You can choose your family. Everyone here has been chosen by someone to be part of our family. And we love you all."

Everyone cheered. Lewis indicated for Arianne to go first as she stood to his left. After that, each person had their turn, some stumbling with things to say, some glowing with happiness, some unsure, but each managed to say something.

By the time it came around to Henley's turn, Isaac had begun to sweat. Typically, Lewis had started at the opposite side of the circle to what they were on, so he'd had to wait for almost everyone else before it got to him.

"I made my first piece of clothing over the last couple of weeks. And I'm happy with how it turned out. I have decided to make a few more pieces before seeing if this is something I want to take further."

Everyone clapped, and Isaac kissed the side of his head. With Henley's flair for design, Isaac had suggested he make some of his own items when he'd once pouted about something not fitting right. Henley had brushed it off until one day they'd revisited the conversation, and Henley had agreed to give it a go. Eventually, Henley was going to get some advice about where to market it because, although they worked in the clothing sector, uniforms were slightly different from more unique and one-off items.

Then it was Isaac's turn. Heart pounding, he said, "Everyone knows I struggled with what to say when I first started doing these. It's difficult to remember the things that went well and so easy to focus on the bad things. But with Henley by my side, that scale is tipping in the other direction, finally." He inhaled and stepped forward, turning to face Henley, whose eyebrows rose. "Henley is the light in my darkness. Every day, he encourages me to be a better person as I do for him. And because of that…" Isaac lowered to one knee, fumbling to remove the box from his pocket as a gasp went around the circle. "I would like to ask Henley to marry me." Isaac opened the purple velvet box as Henley's hands covered his mouth, and his eyes widened. "Will you marry me, sweetheart?"

Henley nodded over and over, tears sliding down his face. He dropped to his knees in front of Isaac, gaze on the ring. Isaac had commissioned a ring that was pure Henley: a white gold band, representing Isaac, being grey and all, and slithers of coloured gems all around the band, to represent Henley and all his many wonderful attributes. When Isaac had seen the result, he'd been so overwhelmed that *he'd* cried.

Now, he pulled the ring from its box, dropped the box to the floor and grasped Henley's hand. Finding his ring finger, Isaac slid the band to the base before pressing a kiss to it amidst cheering and whistling from the guests.

"Oh my god!" Henley's wet gaze flicked from his

hand to Isaac's face and back again. He couldn't seem to decide where to look.

Henley threw his arms around Isaac's neck and held him tight, sobbing his heart out. It was a good thing Isaac knew Henley well enough to know they were happy tears. As people broke free of the circle to congratulate them, they were surrounded by all the people who loved them.

"Yay! A wedding to organise! Are you going to make your outfit, Henley?" Arianne nudged her way into their space, kissing their cheeks.

"Oh god! I don't think I could! Talk about stressful!" Henley laughed, wiping his eyes.

"You look a hot mess." Arianne turned to Isaac. "I'm going to borrow your *fiancé* for a moment to get him looking his best. Be right back!" She waved her fingers at Isaac as she pulled Henley away.

Although Isaac would've loved for Henley to stay with him, he knew Arianne was taking Henley to speak with his sisters and dads, probably to make sure he was alright with everything that had happened. That was the only reason why Isaac wouldn't complain.

They had the rest of their lives to make up for a few missing minutes.

Isaac's parents finally made their way over to him, laughing about not being able to get to them before Henley was whisked away.

"I'm so happy for you, darling," his mum said, giving him one of those big hugs that a child was never too old for.

"Thanks, Mum." Isaac turned to his dad, who clapped his shoulder.

"Nicely done. You take care of him, now, okay?" he said, laughing.

"Already do, Dad. Already do." Isaac didn't mention how he took care of Henley. A few close people knew the finer details about their relationship but not everyone. Henley had agreed he didn't feel right calling Isaac, "Daddy," in front of family, so they'd decided that was a hard limit, although occasionally it had slipped out unintentionally. They weren't worried, though. "Have you heard any news from Felicity?" His sister had been called by their surrogate, Shelby, and told to go there as she thought she was having contractions. The baby was due any time now, and Felicity and Van had gone to see her. They were all going to go to the hospital as soon as they had news about whether Shelby was in labour or not.

"No, nothing yet," his mum said.

Half an hour later, Isaac was wondering where they all were when he saw Henley hustling towards him. His makeup had been redone, and he looked as gorgeous as ever. Isaac didn't mind whether Henley wore makeup or not, it was whatever Henley wanted to do.

When Henley stopped in front of him, biting his lip, Isaac grew concerned. "Is everything okay?"

"Yes. I..." Henley exhaled, nodded and inhaled again. "You beat me to the punch earlier. I hadn't planned on proposing today, but I had the ring ready for when I did. I sent Ariel to go get it for me." Isaac's eyebrows rose as Henley lifted his hand. "I don't know if it's going to fit but..." Henley opened his fingers, showing a white gold band with a yellow gold stripe around the edge.

Now it was Isaac's turn to be shocked. His smile grew as Henley reached for Isaac's hand and slid the ring on his finger. It was a little loose, but they could get that altered, no problem.

"Thank you, sweet boy." He cupped Henley's face, staring into his eyes, and pressed kisses to his forehead, his nose, each cheek and his lips. After, he smoothed his hands around Henley's back and crushed him to his chest. Their first kiss as fiancés.

They pulled apart when a throat cleared right next to them. Isaac blinked a couple of times before focusing on Dad and Pops. "Congratulations, boys. I know you will be very happy."

"Thank you, Dad, Pops." Henley gave them each a soft hug before Isaac followed suit.

"And you've made us happy, too," Pops said, smiling at Lewis as he held onto him.

Would you like the next book in the series? Spoil Me, Daddy, Book 3 follows Aaron and Zaire as Aaron helps Zaire to figure out how to balance the different aspects of his life and become happy with who he is.

Sign up to my newsletter to get a free Crush

prequel short story, Love Conquers and a serial newsletter story every month.

If you have a moment, would you write a review for Soothe Me, Daddy please? Reviews help other readers decide whether they would like to read the book, and therefore, are also important for authors.

# ACKNOWLEDGEMENTS

I want to thank several people who have helped me get this book ready to go:

Emma, thank you so much for believing in me and being my cheerleader. You are amazing.

Maria, my fantastic editor, who helps me keep things straight, gives me advice when I'm lost and an ear when I need it. Keep strong. You're the best.

Renee, who keeps me on the straight and narrow with her evilly helpful deeds. I don't think I would have been able to make everything run as smoothly without you by my side.

# ABOUT ELOUISE EAST

I am Elouise East but feel free to call me Elli. I write sweet and steamy connections in gay romance. I also touch on taboo stories under the name Elouise R East.

Books that tell the stories where friendship and family are the focal point - be it blood family or chosen - is very important to me. That's why I include a variety of personalities, talents, ages, situations and abilities as I believe a story needs, or a character needs. I want my characters to be real, to be relatable, to be free to have whatever views they tell me they have. And trust me, most of the time, I do not have *any* say in the matter!

My characters come to life on the page for me as well as my readers. Their stories unfold in front of me, and I have very little input into how they want to be shown. Just like real life, the lives of my characters change with every choice, every interaction and every conversation. And I wouldn't have it any other way.

I write books that are emotionally realistic, even if liberties are taken with other aspects of my stories. I don't know any other way to write. It comes from deep inside.

Who am I? A single parent to two children who

make life worth living. An avid reader who still devours every book she can get her hands on. A student of learning about any subject that takes her fancy. An author of books she would read herself. And a romantic at heart who loves anything cheesy.

Who's in?

⟵————————⟶

Stalk me here… ;-)
https://elouiseeast.com/
https://elouiseeast.com/newsletter
https://linktr.ee/elouiseeastauthor

Check out https://elouiseeast.com/books for my books!

# BOOKS BY ELOUISE EAST

## DADDY

Love Me, Daddy

Soothe Me, Daddy

Spoil Me, Daddy

## CRUSH

First Kiss

Instant Desire

Primary Seduction

Deep Down

A Crush for Christmas

Life Support

Covert Strength

Love Scene

Lawful Attraction

## CLUB ROYAL

Royal Firsts

Rogue Royal

Secretive Royal

Grieving Royal

Disowned Royal

Trained Royal

Awakened Royal

Commanding Royal

---

## LOVE IN FLAMES

Out of the Frying Pan

Smokescreen

Breathing Fire

---

## JUST A LITTLE CRUSH

Star-Crossed

He's Behind You

A Special Love (newsletter story)

---

## DARK & DIVERGENT

A Biker Make Three

Forbidden Temptation

Too Many Secrets

---

## **<u>STANDALONE</u>**

Treehouse Whispers

9 781915 638304